Book Two
The Summer of Magic Quartet

Dance of the Stones

Andrea Spalding

Orca Book Publishers

National Library of Canada Cataloguing in Publication
Spalding, Andrea.
  Dance of the stones / Andrea Spalding.

(The summer of magic quartet; bk. 2)

ISBN 1-55143-268-4

I. Title. II. Series: Spalding, Andrea. Summer of magic quartet; bk 2.

PS8587. P213D36 2003   jC813'.54   C2003-910057-X

PZ7. S7319Da 2003

First published in the United States, 2003

Library of Congress Control Number: 2003100407

Summary: In Book Two of *The Summer of Magic Quartet*, the four children from *The White Horse Talisman* seek Ava's circlet, buried within the ancient stone circle of Avebury.

Orca Book Publishers gratefully acknowledges the support for its publishing programs provided by the following agencies: the Government of Canada through the Book Publishing Industry Development Program (BPIDP), the Canada Council for the Arts, and the British Columbia Arts Council.

Cover design: Christine Toller
Cover and interior illustrations: Martin Springett
Printed and bound in Canada

IN CANADA:
Orca Book Publishers
P.O Box 5626 Stn. B
Victoria, BC Canada
V8R 6S4

IN THE UNITED STATES:
Orca Book Publishers
PO Box 468
Custer, WA   USA
98240-0468

07 06 05 • 5 4 3

Old English Circle Dance

(danced by the author as a child)

Honor your partners.
Circle to the left (16 steps).
Circle to the right (16 steps).
Circle left again (8 steps).
Circle right again (8 steps).
Men to the middle, clap, then back.
Women to the middle, clap, then back.
Swing your partners, leave women in the middle.
Women circle left, while men circle right.
Men circle left, while women circle right.
Find your partner, everybody swing.
Grand Promenade around the Circle.

Acknowledgements

Many people help in the creation of a book.

Sincere thanks to Kathy for taking us around Avebury and sharing modern archeological thinking with us; to Terry the Druid for sharing his love of the Stones; to Gavin and Janet for the car and hospitality; to Penny for comments; to Jock for bailing me out with the computer; to Maggie and the Orca pod for making it all happen; and, as always, to Dave for ongoing support and background research.

NOTE: Celtic spelling was used for two names in the story. "Myrddin" is pronounced "merthin" and "Hewll" is pronounced "hewl. "Traa dy liooar," which is pronounced "trae de lure" and means "time enough, and "Lhiat myr hoilloo," which is pronounced "lee-at mur hoylew" and means "to thee as thou deservest," are phrases in Manx, the Gaelic language of the Isle of Man.

TABLE OF CONTENTS

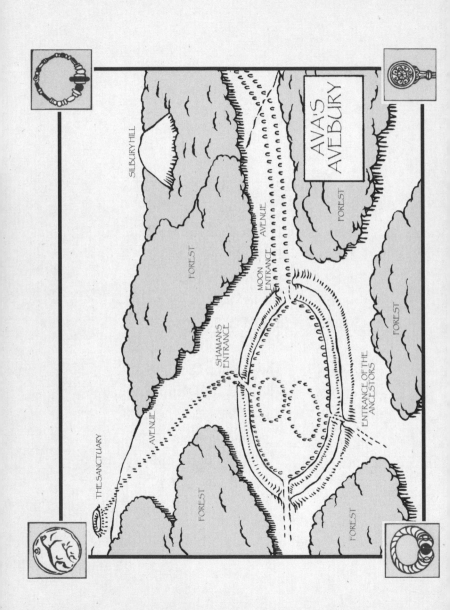

AVA'S
AVEBURY

SILBURY HILL

FOREST

FOREST

FOREST

FOREST

FOREST

THE SANCTUARY

AVENUE

MOON
AVENUE

SHAMAN'S
ENTRANCE

MOON
ENTRANCE

ENTRANCE OF THE
ANCESTORS

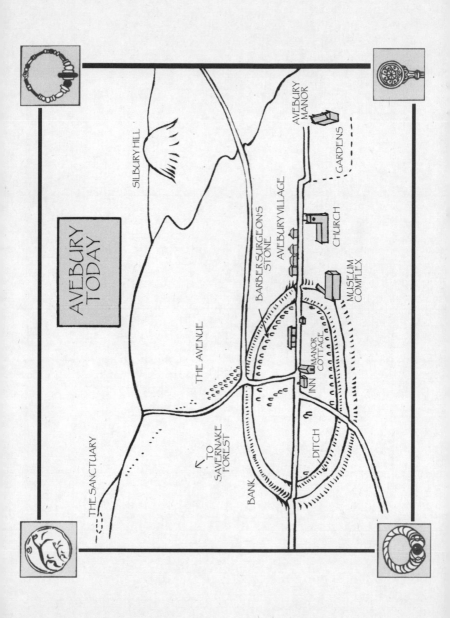

AVEBURY
TODAY

SILBURY HILL

AVEBURY MANOR

GARDENS

THE AVENUE

BARBER SURGEON'S STONE

AVEBURY VILLAGE

CHURCH

MUSEUM COMPLEX

THE SANCTUARY

TO SAVERNAKE FOREST

BANK

DITCH

INN

MANOR COTTAGE

I.
HONOR YOUR PARTNERS

Dawn broke and magic filled the air. Deep in the heart of England, strange things stirred.

The first sunbeam darted through a stand of ancient forest and lit the trunk of a centuries-old oak. For one shining second the features of a face appeared in the bark. Green eyes flashed as the sunbeam passed and the features faded.

Deeper in the forest, a wild boar yawned. The sunbeam glanced off wicked teeth and tusks. The mouth closed. The beam moved on and the boar melted once more into shadowland.

The second sunbeam slid across the downs and kissed a conical green mound that swelled up, apart from the other hills. Only the lark that rose from its nest on the summit heard the greeting from the ancient king beneath. The lark wove the greeting into its song to welcome the sun.

The third sunbeam shot its magical light into a valley. There towered a Stone Circle, great gray stones veiled in morning mist. The golden beam lit the dew-covered grass.

The dew became a carpet of flashing diamonds. The dancing light pierced the mist veil and caught a night-prowling wraith, forever struggling to enter the Circle. The wraith fought the light, seeking shelter in the shadows between the stones. The light triumphed. Veils of mist swirled, and the figure dissolved.

The tide of light flooded and washed each Sarsen Stone. The stones were ready. As gray became gold, the largest stone spun on its axis, then stood sentinel as before.

The magic happened quickly, without a witness. That was to change. Four ordinary children were about to be called to the Circle.

⬡

The Wise Ones watched the Earthdawn from their place among the stars.

As the first stone stirred, Ava's cry of happiness shivered the sky.

"The stone has turned! My magic is ripening at last. It's time to call the children." Ava stretched her wings "Myrddin, Equus, join me. Send blessings down to Gaia. Old Magic stirs with each new dawn, but the Dark Magic also grows. Help give the human children strength to resist one while embracing the other."

"Light and Dark, Dark and Light," rumbled Myrddin. "Children, may you learn that one will always bring the other on its coattails." He spread his arms and shook out his cloak of hidden colors. A shower of stardust sparkled and fell on the blue planet below.

"Light and Dark, Dark and Light," murmured Equus.

He shook his mane and stamped his hoof. A fiery star streaked the dawn-washed sky. "Children, may you seek strength from the light and be unafraid of the dark."

"Light and Dark, Dark and Light," whispered Ava. She spread her magnificent wings and her hawk-like beauty shone unchecked, dimming the stars of the Milky Way. "Children, the time is near. The light calls as the darkness gathers. May its circle always protect you."

Ava soared upwards and spun a rainbow that circled the setting moon.

The four children were sleeping.

The golden finger of dawn sneaked through a gap in the curtain and touched one child's face. Owen Maxwell woke instantly. He swung carefully out of his upper bunk to avoid disturbing his Canadian cousin Adam in the bunk below. He padded across the floorboards and pulled aside the curtain. "Weird light," he muttered as he hung out of the open window to see better.

The rising sun blazed from the horizon on one side of White Horse Farm, and the setting moon gleamed on the other. A brief shower blew over the ground, releasing earthy aromas, and suddenly the moon was framed by a rainbow. High above hung the bright morning star.

A shiver went up Owen's spine.

"Is this it?" he called softly. "Wise Ones, is this the star message you promised to send us? Is it time for our next adventure?"

The cry of a hawk was the only answer.

Owen squinted up into the light.

The hawk circled below the morning star. The circles became wider and wider as she dipped closer to the earth. As the hawk banked one way she was bathed in gold; as she banked the other way she was washed with silver.

"Awesome," breathed Owen. He held his breath.

The hawk folded her wings and plummeted like a stone toward the pasture.

Owen gasped.

In the same second the sun leaped into the sky. The banished moon fell below the horizon and the morning star faded.

Only the hawk remained, hurtling toward the ground. Within centimeters of the earth she unleashed her talons and spread her wings. Wingtips brushed grass. Razor-sharp claws stretched and grabbed. The hawk swooped up with the tawny body of a weasel hanging in her deadly grip. She flapped heavily toward the nearest patch of woodland and disappeared with her prey.

Light and Dark, Dark and Light. The light grows but dark things waken. Ava's words were transferred thoughts, but they filled Owen's head as loudly and clearly as true speech. *The stones have stirred. Tell the others. The time is near for the Circle Dance.*

"Adam . . . Adam . . . WAKE UP," Owen hissed in his cousin's ear. He shook Adam's shoulder.

Adam squinted at the dawn light, pulled a face and tried to burrow under his pillow. "Too early."

"Adam, it's happening. Ava spoke to me."

Adam's eyes shot open. "YOU heard from the Wise Ones?"

Owen nodded, his eyes dancing.

Adam rolled out of bed. He stood in the middle of the room, rumpled and annoyed. "Why you? What did they say?"

"I'm getting the girls. I'll be back." Owen lifted the catch on the bedroom door and disappeared down the corridor.

Adam ran to the window and stared up at the sky. Everything seemed normal. His eyes scanned the hills beyond White Horse Farm. In Canada, where he and Chantel lived, they would have been called hills, but his English cousins called them the downs. Carved into the downs was the gigantic figure of a white horse. It had been cut through the grass to the white chalk beneath over three thousand years ago. The carving had started their adventures.

Chantel's and my adventure, thought Adam resentfully. If he and Chantel hadn't come to visit from Canada, none of it would have happened. He hunched his shoulders. Why were the Wise Ones talking to Owen? It was Adam they should be talking to. They talked to Chantel last time; now it was his turn. Adam gazed up at the chalk carving.

The chalk horse had become Equus, a wise being from the stars. Equus had spoken to Chantel in her dreams. When Chantel had ended up in hospital with a broken leg, she had directed Adam and her two English cousins in helping Equus search for his mate, the Red Mare. They also recovered his magical talisman. By the end of the adventure, all four cousins had met the Wise Ones and promised to help them recover other magical tools.

Adam remembered the exhilaration of the wild ride

through the stars when Equus and the Red Mare had taken all four cousins to the Place Beyond Morning. He remembered his awe at meeting two other Wise Ones, Myrddin, a cloaked man, and Ava, a beautiful being who seemed to be half-woman, half-bird.

Adam trembled as a wave of fear washed over him. Part of the adventure had been terrifying. A terrible dragon had tried to control his mind and make him do dreadful things. Maybe this adventure would be scary too. Maybe they shouldn't get involved. He turned nervously as the bedroom door opened.

Chantel, his seven-year-old sister, hopped in, her leg held up so her cast wouldn't bang on the floor. "Did you speak to the Wise Ones?" she whispered.

"No," said Adam. He pulled out the chair from Owen's desk so she could sit down and rest her leg. "They spoke to Owen."

The door opened again and Owen and his eleven-year-old sister Holly joined them.

"What's up?" Holly hissed.

Owen grinned. "We've had a message from the Wise Ones."

"About time," said Holly. "I was fed up with waiting. What happened?"

"The light woke me. It was really weird," said Owen. "So I hung out of the window to see better. The sun and moon were shining at the same time, and there was a rainbow around the moon and this big star, the morning star I think, between them. Then I spotted a hawk. It circled around in the light, turning silver on one side and gold on the other. It dived toward the earth. I thought it was going to crash, but it caught a weasel . . . "

"Ugh!" Chantel shuddered.

Owen ignored her. " . . . and flapped off to the woods. Then Ava spoke." Owen's voice deepened as he repeated Ava's words. 'Light and Dark, Dark and Light. The light grows but dark things stir. The stones have stirred. Tell the others. The time is near for the Circle Dance.' He paused. "At least I *think* I heard her voice . . . only it wasn't a real voice. It was in my head."

Chantel nodded excitedly. "That's how the Wise Ones speak. It's in your head but as clear as clear." She thought for a moment. "I think they only spoke out loud when we were in the Place Beyond Morning."

Holly agreed.

"Yup, and know what's neat? You can think your answers back. You don't have to speak out loud." Chantel raised her eyebrows at her cousin. "Didn't you do that last time?"

Owen shook his head. "It was you two and Holly who had most of the adventures." He grinned. "I guess it's my turn now."

Adam shifted.

'The stones have stirred. The time is near for the Circle Dance,' quoted Holly. "What's that? What do we have to do?"

Owen shrugged. "Dunno. That's all Ava said."

Chantel hopped up from the chair and held out her hands. "They can speak to us best when we are asleep, but sometimes they spoke if we helped by making a circle. Let's try. I hope Equus will come. I miss riding on him. He hasn't visited my dreams for ages."

"None of them have," Adam grumbled as he grasped his sister's hand and offered his other to Owen. "I've hated waiting."

"Me too," said Holly. "But I sometimes wonder if it really happened."

The other children nodded.

"Well it did happen," said Owen firmly. "Now it's going to happen again. Are you in or out?" He held out his hand toward his older sister.

Holly laughed. "Don't be an idiot. In, of course." She grasped Chantel's and Owen's hands and completed the circle. "Okay, now what?"

A soft knock sounded and the bedroom door creaked open.

Four startled faces turned.

A head appeared. "Good, you're awake."

The children let out their breath.

"Mum, you scared us," said Holly.

"Sorry." Lynne Maxwell looked curiously at the circle.

The cousins hastily dropped hands.

"I didn't mean to interrupt your game." Lynne smiled. "I was coming to wake you. Hurry up and dress. We've an early start this morning. We're going on a trip."

Shock rippled over the children's faces.

"We . . . we are?" stammered Adam.

Lynne pushed the door wide open, carried in four backpacks and dropped them by the bunks. "Your Uncle

Ron got a call late last night. A stud farm in Wiltshire needs his advice for a few days. It's a lovely part of the country and our entire family, including Adam and Chantel, is invited down to stay."

"But we can't leave here," blurted Owen.

His mother's smile faded. "I thought you'd be pleased." She looked puzzled. "You've been moping around like lost dogs for the last few days. I thought you'd jump at the chance to go somewhere else."

Holly spread her hands. "We've made plans, Mum."

"So've we," her mother snapped back. "Sorry we couldn't consult you, but it happened too fast. Most people would give their eyeteeth to spend a week at Avebury."

"A week," gasped Owen. "Seven whole days . . . you're kidding?"

"Where's Avebury?" whispered Chantel to Adam.

Adam shrugged then looked across at his Auntie Lynne. "What if Mom or Dad phone?" he said.

Chantel froze.

Aunt Lynne gazed steadily back at her nephew and niece while Holly and Owen dropped their eyes. Everyone knew that Adam and Chantel's parents wouldn't phone. They were too busy fighting about their divorce. That's why they had shipped Adam and Chantel to England in the first place.

"We will let your mum and dad know where we are and leave a forwarding number on the answering machine in case they forget," said Lynne gently. She put out her hand to pat Adam's shoulder, but he jerked away.

"Avebury?" said Holly after a moment of silence. "My teacher's mentioned Avebury."

"I should think so," said her mother briskly. "It's one of the most important prehistoric sites in England. That's why your dad and I thought you would like to see it. Avebury is much older than the White Horse carving you've all found so fascinating. Five thousand years old, I think."

Owen wasn't listening. He felt as though he would burst with frustration. Just as something magical was about to happen to him, his mother and father made stupid plans. "Mum, can't you and Dad go on your own?" he burst out. "We can stay here. Mr. and Mrs. O'Reilly will look after us. You've done it before."

"Yeah, we don't mind staying. We like spending the summer in Uffington Village," Adam said, jumping in to support his cousin.

Chantel slipped her hand into her aunt's palm. "Do we have to go?" she asked softly.

Lynne looked down at Chantel and across at the other children. "Why can I never second-guess you kids?" She scratched her ear. "Is there something going on that I should know about?"

The children shuffled uneasily but shook their heads.

Lynne shrugged. "Sorry, I thought you'd enjoy it, so we've already accepted the invitation. It would be rude to change our minds now." She pointed to the backpacks. "Pack enough clothes for seven days. Oh, Holly, find three bike helmets. Dad's strapping bikes on the back of the car since you won't be able to ride around on the ponies like you do here." She smiled down at Chantel. "We'll figure out something else for you, Poppet."

Chantel sighed and withdrew her hand.

"Breakfast in fifteen minutes," said Lynne brightly and left.

Owen kicked the chair. "I can't believe Mum and Dad organized that without asking us. How could they? How can we leave when something magic's about to happen?" He looked across at Chantel. "What if you break your other leg? That would fix it."

"Break your own leg," Chantel retorted.

"I'll push you down the stairs if you like," offered Adam.

"You and whose army?" Owen hunkered down into a sumo wrestler stance and beckoned. "Come on. Come on. Try it. Try it!"

"Give over, you two," Holly muttered. "Stop being ten-year-old brats. I'm trying to think."

"Huh. Being eleven means you're not a brat, does it?"

"Oh, do shut up, Owen, I'm trying to remember. Avebury . . . what do I know about Avebury?"

"Who cares?" said Owen. "It's a stupid name for a stupid place." He swung up on his bunk. "I'm on strike. I'm not going anywhere." He disappeared under his duvet.

Chantel giggled.

Holly picked up two backpacks. "He's crazy. Come on, Chantel, let's get out of here," she said and led the way back to her room.

Adam eyed the mound that was Owen. He wasn't sure what to do. He wanted to support his cousin, but didn't want to anger his aunt and uncle. "Are you really on strike?" he asked.

The mound heaved and Owen stuck out his head. "Fat

chance." He grinned. "I've got a better idea. 'Don't get mad, get even!' Let's make them so sorry they've taken us away, we'll be brought home faster than a speeding bullet."

"You mean Operation Irritation?" Adam laughed. "I'm good at that."

Owen jumped off the bunk with a thud and ran over to the laundry hamper.

"What are you doing?" Adam asked as dirty laundry flew through the air.

"Packing," retorted Owen. "First find smelly socks, preferably odd ones. Dad won't notice, but it gets Mum really choked."

Dawn Magic coursed through the stones, growing stronger as the day progressed.

Outwardly still gray monoliths, inwardly the stones were stirring. First a spreading warmth at their centers. Then a flutter as light as the beat of a butterfly wing. The flutter became a pulse. The magic coursed faster and the stones shimmered with energy. Deep inside each one, a heart began to beat.

The journey in the station wagon was tense.

Uncle Ron and Aunt Lynne kept up a stream of cheerful chatter. The four cousins slumped in their seats and answered in monosyllables.

Finally, Uncle Ron pulled to the side of the road and switched off the engine. He swung around and glared. "That's it, you four! Now, what's up?"

The children dropped their eyes.

"Look at me," he roared.

Four sets of eyes widened and flicked upward.

"We are going to Avebury. We are going for a week. I'm working there. Mope if you like, but I expect politeness to me, your mum and our hosts, the Prendergasts. Understood?"

Four heads nodded.

Ron Maxwell fixed a steely eye on the two girls hunched in the back seat. "Holly and Chantel, stop the 'go slow'! Chantel has been whizzing around, despite the cast on her leg, until this morning."

Chantel flushed and Holly bit her lip.

Ron turned his attention to the middle seat. "Owen, spare me your idea of humor. If you wish to wear the odor-iferous clothing you've stuffed in your backpack, that's your choice. But stay outside and don't inflict yourself on anyone else. Rain or shine, you eat all your meals on the back step until you find a washing machine."

Adam gave a snort of laughter that he changed into a cough as his uncle frowned.

"Turn off your watch alarm, Adam. I will not be sub-jected to bleeps every five minutes. Or, of course, you can hand it over."

Adam frantically started reprogramming.

"And the next person who sings 'Ninety-nine Bottles of Beer on the Wall' will get out and walk," Lynne interjected.

The kids smothered grins.

Lynne pushed the hair out of her eyes and sighed. "I don't get it. Why are you all so angry? We thought you would enjoy seeing the Stone Circle at Avebury."

There was a sharp intake of breath. "What? Where are you and Dad taking us?" Owen asked.

"The Avebury Stone Circle . . . you must have heard of it?"

Holly leaned forward and poked Owen. "That's it! I remember," she said urgently. "Avebury's a Stone Circle that's older than Stonehenge." She took a breath. "And guess what? The old name for a circle of stones is a dance!"

The cousins exchanged looks.

"A circle," said Owen. He leaned forward and hung over the front seat between his parents. His voice wobbled. "You and Dad are taking us to . . . to see a Stone Circle?"

Lynne nodded. "We are going to stay at Manor Cottage, right in the middle of the Circle."

"How soon before we get there?" said Owen.

Holly, Adam and Chantel leaned back in their seats and laughed until tears poured down their cheeks.

"I give up." Lynne threw up her hands. "Ron, ignore them. Just drive to Avebury."

2.
FORES† MAGIC

"*They're on their way,*" *said Ava.* "*Soon the children will be able to perform the ritual and I will reclaim my circlet.*"

Myrddin frowned. "*We need more than the ritual to help us. Each day the Dark Being moves closer. Already her influence is felt the length and breadth of the Milky Way. Dark things grow stronger. Her supporters are legion. We are few.*" *He shook his cloak restlessly.* "*We erred when we removed our tools of power from the Place Beyond Morning and hid them on Gaia.*"

"*The tools have been safe for aeons,*" *said Equus.*

Myrddin moved edgily. "*I know, I know, but I am fearful. It will take the human children time to recover Ava's circlet. Then there is still my staff to find and the Lady to waken.*"

Ava laid a wingtip on his arm. "'*Traa dy liooar,*' *the Lady said.* '*Time enough.*' *Remember?*"

"*I remember,*" *said Myrddin.* "*I remember a time when the Silver Citadel and the Place Beyond Morning were the* symbols of all that was good. I remember when Gaia was young and the human people innocent. I remember when we were honored and first named Wise Ones for giving up our tools of power. I remember when we believed that hiding our tools would make the Dark Being leave us in peace." Myrddin spread his arms wide. "All for naught. Now she threatens to destroy everything, and the humans have forgotten us." He shook his head. "Only four children hear us. How can we tell children of the horror that the Dark Being has become."

"We will tell them gently, bit by bit," said Equus.

"They have hidden strength," said Ava. "They helped Equus regain his talisman. Rejoice, Myrddin. The first task is completed and the second has begun. The dark things stir as the Dark Being approaches, but followers of light stir also. The stones turned, Myrddin! The dawn light woke them to help us. Dark and Light, Light and Dark. Step by step we will balance the darkness, but only if we keep faith with the light."

The Maxwell family's station wagon sped across country, cresting the downs, then dipping into wide green valleys. The day became hot and oppressive. The children wound down the windows and let the air stream past their faces. Suddenly the terrain changed. They drove through a cool green tunnel formed by branches meeting overhead.

"Look at the trees," gasped Holly. "That one's gigantic." She pointed to a gnarled, moss-covered oak. Its twisted trunk leaned out over a high bank and overhung the road.

Her father slowed the car. "We're driving through Savernake Forest, one of the oldest stretches of oak forest in England. This is a royal forest where kings and queens used to hunt for deer. That tree was probably growing in the Middle Ages, five or six hundred years ago."

"Cool," said Adam. "We've got some old trees on the West Coast of Canada. They're called Douglas firs." He looked at some of the oaks. "They're way taller."

"Why is everything bigger and better in Canada?" said Owen.

His mother turned and glared. Owen rolled his eyes.

Adam subsided, a hurt look on his face.

Ron drove into a small car park. "We've been sitting too long. Let's look at the oaks and run off some energy."

"Yes." Owen and Adam tumbled out of the car.

Owen punched Adam's arm in an unspoken apology. "Beat you to that tree over there." The two boys raced across the car park and leaped into the undergrowth. Bulldozing their way through ferns and deadfall, they argued at the top of their lungs about which tree looked the oldest.

Holly paused in a patch of green light filtering through the branches above her. The forest was beautiful, so much bigger and more mysterious than the woods near her house. She sniffed, pulling the heady smell of loamy soil, damp mossy banks and the sharp odor of acorns deep into her lungs. Inside her a feeling grew. This place was special. Holly plunged into the tangle of bracken.

Chantel sighed. It wasn't fair. Everyone was leaving her behind again. When she first broke her leg, they had all helped her. Even her brother had been nice to her. But now they expected her to do everything for herself. She gave a little sniff while struggling to extract her crutches from the car.

"I'm sorry. This isn't an easy place for you to explore," Uncle Ron said as he came round to help her.

"It's okay," Chantel said without conviction.

"We can use the trail," Aunt Lynne suggested.

Chantel nodded. "I'm good on crutches but not in this." She poked one crutch into a mass of undergrowth beside the car park. "I'd be tangled up forever."

Uncle Ron patted her shoulder and strode vigorously ahead.

Lynne chuckled. "Your uncle always needs to speed walk to work out driving kinks." She laughed. "He hates sitting for any length of time. Owen is just like him." She looked quizzically at Chantel. "That leaves you and me. Shall we walk up the path together?"

"Sure, if you think you can keep up with me." Chantel grinned and set off, swinging her crutches at a great pace.

"Hey, look at us," Owen and Adam hollered and waved from their perch on a giant branch.

Chantel and Lynne waved back.

Holly never turned her head.

For once, practical Holly was in a world all her own. The ancient forest captivated her. She closed her ears to the distant sounds of traffic and her family and imagined she was walking alone. The bracken and brambles were waist high, but she thrust them aside in a swimming motion. The green light enveloped her, dragging her onward as though she was caught in the current of a deep, green river. The first tree she had spotted, the twisted oak overhanging the road, drew her like a magnet. Finally, breathless and scratched, she washed up on its tangle of roots and gazed at the bulky black trunk.

I was right, you're really, really old, thought Holly as she clambered over the thick tracery of roots. She reached the trunk and fingered the fissures etched deep in the bark. Small ferns and clumps of grass sprouted from the hollows, miniature hanging gardens that gave the tree a festive air as though it had pinned on jewelry. Just above her head, the trunk split into three massive limbs. From them sprang a web of branches holding up a dense umbrella of greenery.

I could hide up there, Holly thought. No one would ever find me. The branches are so big there must be lots of places to sit.

She swung up and straddled a branch.

Greenery enclosed her, branches embraced her and Holly became part of the tree. The leaves whispered to each other, small birds hopped around unafraid and a continuous buzz of insects hung in the air.

She gazed upward. High above hung a pale green ball of leaves that seemed to glow. It was a bunch of magical mistle-toe. Holly gazed at it in awe.

Suddenly a breeze blew and a flutter of red caught her eye. Someone had tied a piece of plastic tape to a lower branch. "Ugh," said Holly. She edged along her branch, stretched and tugged. The tape snapped off. She rolled it up and stowed it in her jeans pocket.

Holly crawled back and leaned forward against the main trunk. She stretched her arms as wide as she could. They circled only a fraction of the tree's width. "You're amazing," she whispered, her cheek against the bark. "You must be the oldest tree here."

"I am," the tree whispered back.

Startled, Holly drew back, then grinned and looked around. "Good one," she chuckled. "Show yourself, Owen, wherever you are!"

No answer. Her smile faded.

"Come on," she called sharply. "Stop trying to scare me. It's not funny."

Still no one answered.

Puzzled, Holly checked below the oak but saw no one. She climbed farther up the trunk, slithered out on the branch that leaned over the road, and peeped through the leaves. Nobody was hiding below the bank.

Then she heard Owen and Adam calling each other, way back in the forest.

Holly edged back to the massive trunk and leaned against it. She shook her head to clear it. "Trees can't speak," she muttered.

"They speak." The whisper hung in the air. "But humans never hear."

"Then why can I hear you?" replied Holly, hesitantly. She looked around to try and identify where the voice was coming from.

"You have walked in the Place Beyond Morning." The whisper surrounded her.

Holly gasped. "How do you know?"

"Stardust shines in your hair."

Holly grabbed a handful of dark curls. She pulled them in front of her face and squinted. They looked perfectly normal. She let go. "Who *are* you?"

"The oldest oak. The Mother Tree. And you?"

"Holly."

The tree gave a deep chuckle, and Holly felt the branch tremble.

"No wonder you hear Treespeak. You are named for one of the Great Trees. Oak, Ash, Yew, Beech, Hawthorn, Holly and Ivy, magic trees all."

"I thought I was named for Christmas. My birthday's in December." Holly stroked the trunk as she spoke.

"Holly is older than Christmas. In the beginning was the Old Magic. Holly boughs strewn at entrances celebrate the Greenwood and keep Dark Magic at bay."

"Goodness!" said Holly in awe.

"Holly, HOLLY. Time to go." Her father's voice echoed through the forest.

"My dad's calling."

"One moment, child. Dark things stir. My forest labors under siege. Will you help me?"

"If I can," said Holly, not sure how she could help a tree miles away from anywhere.

"Thank you. In return for your kindness I offer gifts. Hold out your hand, child."

Holly obeyed. An acorn dropped into her palm.

"Keep safe this acorn, young Holly Berry. It holds the power of the Greenwood. So does my mistletoe. In times of need you may take some."

"Thank you," said Holly politely.

"I also offer words of power, for protection against wickedness."

"Okay," said Holly, mystified. She tucked the acorn in the bottom of her pocket, beneath the tape.

"Bend your ear to my trunk, for words of power must never be uttered lest needed."

Holly leaned into the trunk.

The whisper came from deep within the tree. She had to strain to hear, and what she heard made no sense.

"Lhiat myr hoilloo."

"Pardon?" said Holly.

"Lhiat myr hoilloo."

"Lee-at mur hoylew," repeated Holly under her breath. "What does it mean?"

"'Tis Oldspeak for 'to thee as thou deservest.' Treasure the words deep in your heart."

"HOLLY!"

"Coming," Holly shouted. She patted the tree trunk. "I have to go . . . but I will look after your acorn and . . . and remember the words. Thank you for your gifts."

"May your leaves be ever green," the oak rustled.

Bemused, Holly swung down to the ground and picked her way across the maze of roots. Her mind racing, she retraced her trail through the forest.

***

Ron drove the final miles toward Avebury. The hot air was thick and heavy. He rubbed his forehead. "There's a storm hanging around."

"Hurry up rain, freshen the air," joked Lynne. As she

spoke, heavy drops of rain spattered on the windscreen.

"Well done, Mum," said Owen. "The weather was listening."

With the rain came relief from the heat. Irritations forgotten, everyone except Holly chatted happily about the forest and the size of the trees.

Holly gazed unseeing out the window.

"Holly, where did you get to?" Owen asked eventually.

"To the Mother Tree," Holly replied.

"The Mother Tree?" repeated Lynne. "What's that, the oldest tree in the forest?"

"Yes," Holly muttered, looking uncomfortable.

"How did you know? Was there a plaque?" her mum continued.

Holly flushed. "No. I . . . er . . . just guessed."

"No way," Owen crowed. "I think our tree was the oldest, don't you, Adam?"

To Holly's relief, the conversation flowed away from her. She slipped her hand into her pocket and pulled out the acorn.

Chantel touched her knee. "You okay?"

Holly nodded. She passed the acorn to Chantel. "Does this look like anything special?"

Chantel examined it. "An acorn! I've never seen a real one before. They don't grow in Alberta."

The boys turned round to see what she was looking at.

"Can I see?" Adam grabbed the acorn. It slipped out of his fingers, hit the floor and rolled out of sight.

"That's mine and if you've lost it, you're in big trouble." Holly's voice was fierce.

"Keep your hair on. It's only an acorn. Besides, I didn't

mean to drop it." Adam had the grace to look ashamed.

"You were snatching," accused Chantel.

"What's the matter now?" called Lynne from the front seat.

"Nothing, just dropped something," Holly said, looking daggers at Adam.

Lynne sighed. "I'm sure you'll find it when we stop."

"De poor liddle girl's lost her acorn. Oo, don't cry," mocked Owen, offering Holly a filthy hankie.

Holly pushed his hand away. "We'd better find it," she hissed at Adam. "It's special. It's from the oldest tree."

Adam and Owen stared.

Holly glared back at them.

Adam's eyes dropped first. "Okay . . . okay . . . I'll help you look as soon as we stop."

"We're nearly there," called Ron. "Watch for Silbury and then we are not far from the Stone Circle."

"That is." Lynne pointed.

A large conical green mound rose up beside the road.

Ron slowed the car.

"It's big, but *what* is it?" persisted Adam. He wound down the window so everyone could see without rain streaks.

"Nobody knows. Silbury Hill is one of the great mysteries of the world," said Ron. "It's a man-made hill, the biggest ancient man-made structure in Europe. It's several thousand years old. But no one has any idea why it was constructed."

"There are lots of stories," added Lynne. "The best is that it's the burial mound of King Sel, the Golden King. He is supposed to have been buried with his horse and a complete set of golden armor."

"Sweet," said Adam.

"Unfortunately, no one has ever been able to find his grave, though the mound has been tunneled into several times," Lynne finished.

"I'm glad," said Chantel dreamily. "It's much nicer to think of him still being there."

Ron turned the car off the highway and they bumped down a narrow lane. "Watch for the stones," he called.

✶✶✶✶

The stones stood gray, wet and silent. They towered over umbrellaed tourists who, despite the rain, patted them, photographed them and walked slowly and admiringly around the mile circumference of the Great Circle.

Suddenly there was a quiver in the air, a tiny shiver of delight, as the clouds concealing the sun parted.

A station wagon was approaching the Circle entrance at the head of the Avenue, the entrance the stones knew as the Shaman's Entrance.

The children had arrived.

✶✶✶✶

As Ron spoke, the rain stopped and shafts of sunlight lit two standing stones, one on each side of the road. As the car passed between, a double rainbow arched overhead.

"What a welcome," said Lynne as they swept into the small village of Avebury.

The wide-eyed children said nothing. They were watching a hawk circling.

Ron eased the car between narrow gateposts and drove into

a graveled courtyard. He stopped and stretched.

"My acorn," hissed Holly. "Watch your feet."

Adam unfastened his seat belt and slid to the floor. He stretched his arm under the seat and flailed around until his fingers touched the small woody object. He pulled it out and, without a word, handed it to Holly.

Holly smiled with relief and stuffed the acorn in her pocket. "Thanks."

Harmony restored, the four children tumbled out of the car and gazed around.

Manor Cottage was a large stone house on the main street of a tiny village.

The children ran out into the street and looked up and down.

"This place is smaller than Uffington," Adam said. "I didn't think it was possible."

"Great things come in small parcels," remarked a man with a long, gray beard. He strode past holding a tall, carved wooden stick with an ornate brass top.

Adam stared, then colored with embarrassment.

"Keep your voice down," hissed Owen. "There are people around."

"Strange people," Chantel whispered back.

The children watched as the gray-bearded man was joined by a long-haired woman in a flowing dress. An enormous crystal pendant hung around her neck.

Other people were sitting on walls, enjoying the sunshine. Many were tourists. The car park next to Manor Cottage was filled with buses, and the old inn beyond was doing a roaring trade. Village people bustled to and fro carrying shopping bags or clutching letters to mail.

The doors of the village shops were propped open. A gift shop, an antique shop and a tiny grocery store-cum-post office sat in a row opposite Manor Cottage. Then came a field with a stile in the fence used by a constant stream of visitors entering and exiting. The field was followed by another row of gray stone buildings, obviously houses. Flowers bloomed in pots and window boxes, and all the roofs sported well-trimmed thatch.

On the other side of Manor Cottage was a collection of large barns with an arrow on the side that proclaimed MUSEUM. Beyond, a church spire loomed over a wall, and in the distance a large old house was half hidden behind a row of trees.

"It's tiny, but pretty," said Chantel softly. "I like it here."

"Mum," called Owen, "where's the rest of the Circle? I only spotted two stones as we drove in."

Lynne walked out of the courtyard to join them. She waved her arm in a big gesture. "We're in the middle of it. The Circle is large; it surrounds the village. The stones are in the fields beyond the houses." She pointed to a woman climbing the stile across the road. "Half the Circle is on that side and half on this. Unload your stuff from the car and you can go and explore."

"Lynne, Ron. How nice to see you again! I thought I heard the car." A tall dark woman came out of the back door as the children started pulling their belongings from the car. She hugged Lynne and shook Ron's hand. "We are so grateful you could come at short notice." She turned and looked at the children. "This must be your family."

Lynne gestured. "Mrs. Prendergast, meet Holly and Owen."

They shook hands.

"And Adam and Chantel, Ron's brother's children."

"Hi," said Chantel shyly. Adam thrust out his hand, copying Owen.

"Welcome to England," said Mrs. Prendergast, then led the way through the open door, talking to Lynne over the children's heads. "Come and see the rooms. We often rent this cottage during the summer, so everything's in order. I've put the girls in the ground floor bedroom. There's a bathroom downstairs as well as up so it will be nice and easy for Chantel. The boys have the front room upstairs, and you have the room at the back. I've left basic groceries in the fridge so you should have everything you need."

Carrying their backpacks, the children followed the adults.

"Our room has French doors leading to the garden." Holly ran across the bedroom and flung them open. She stepped out from the back of the house onto a sunlit patio containing pots filled with brightly colored plants. A path ran from the patio across an expanse of lawn.

Chantel followed. "There's a gate at the end of the garden."

A rapping on the bedroom door interrupted them.

"Can we come in?" called Owen.

Holly ran back inside and opened the door.

The boys rushed through and leapt onto the nearest bed, pushing and shoving each other.

"Hey, that's my bed," complained Chantel. "Mess it, you make it."

Adam blew a raspberry.

Owen laughed. He somersaulted onto the pillow and finished upside down in a headstand, his legs against the wall. "So what's the big mystery about the acorn, Sis?" he asked, his face going red as he concentrated on keeping his balance.

"Don't call me Sis," Holly said, playing for time. She wanted to hug the Forest Magic to herself a little longer.

Owen grinned. "Sorry, Holly!" he chanted.

Adam and Chantel chuckled.

Holly tried to change the subject. "We've got our own entrance, look. We can sneak out at night." She pointed to the French doors and the path down to the garden gate.

"Come on Holly . . . what's with the acorn?"

Holly gave up, knowing that Owen would give her no peace. "You're not the only one who got a magic message today. So did I. A tree spoke to me."

"What?" Owen collapsed, landing on Adam in a tangle of legs and arms.

"Thought that would get you," said Holly.

Chantel's eyes widened. "One of the oak trees?"

Holly nodded. "Yes, the Mother Tree."

Adam pushed Owen off his chest. "Wild! What did it say?"

"Not a lot. Dad called and I had to leave," Holly admitted. "But it sounded anxious. It worried about dark things stirring and I said I'd help if I could. Then it told me to keep its acorn safe 'cause it holds the power of the Greenwood. Oh, and it knew I'd been to the Place Beyond Morning. It saw stardust in my hair!"

Everyone stared at Holly's head.

Laughing, Holly covered her curls with her hands.

"I thought it was dandruff," said Owen, deadpan.

Holly grinned but refused to be baited. "Anyway, that's why I was mad when Adam dropped the acorn."

"Can I see it again?" Adam asked.

Holly pulled the acorn out of her pocket and handed it over.

Adam examined it carefully, then handed it to Owen.

"Looks ordinary," Owen said. "What's it supposed to do?"

Holly shrugged. "No idea."

"Ask the Wise Ones," said Adam. He grinned and pointed to a shrub growing beside the patio. "Or maybe a twig will tell you."

Holly ignored him. "There's more. The tree gave me permission to use its mistletoe, and it taught me some words of power."

"Mistletoe. That's really useful. Christmas is only six months away," said Owen sarcastically. "So, go on. What are the words of power?"

Holly looked uncomfortable. "I don't know if I'm supposed to tell," she muttered.

"Of course you are . . . we're all in this together," Owen protested. "We might need words of power to help Ava."

"Holly's right. Words of power can be misused." Adam unexpectedly supported Holly.

Everyone stared at him and he flushed. "They shouldn't be said out loud in case something evil is listening," he persisted. "Remember when we were looking for the talisman? The dragon wanted me to use words of power to set him free forever."

Chantel shuddered. "That would have been awful."

A long silence fell as everyone relived Chantel's narrow escape.

"Tell you what," said Holly finally. "If we take a solemn oath not to misuse the words, I'll show you. I'll write them down. But you must promise never to say the words unless you really, really need to."

"That's fair," agreed Owen.

"We promise," chanted Chantel and Adam.

Holly tore a page from a notepad beside the bed and wrote down the phrase, just as it sounded. *Lee-at mur hoylew. To thee as thou deservest.* She showed everyone.

Owen and Adam burst out laughing.

"No wonder you didn't want to say it," sputtered Owen.

"What language is this?" grinned Adam.

"Mother Tree called it Oldspeak. It's probably spelled wrong, but that's what it sounded like."

Owen snatched the paper and began rolling the words around his tongue. "Leeat . . . "

Holly clapped her hand over his mouth. "OWEN!!"

"Mmm." Owen pulled back. "I'm sorry . . . I forgot. I won't do it again, I promise." Owen's lips moved silently as he committed the phrase to memory then thrust the paper at Adam.

There was silence as everyone in turn memorized the magic words.

"We'd better take a vow never to tell," said Chantel as she handed the paper back to Holly.

"And you all better keep it," muttered Holly, looking daggers at Owen.

The children stood up, clasped right hands in the center of the circle and crossed their chests with their left hands, while chanting:

Cross my heart and hope to die,
Should I ever tell a lie.
I made a promise not to tell.
If I do, I'll go to hell.

"Ava said dark things are stirring," Owen remarked as they dropped hands. "So did your tree."

"Two messages," said Chantel after a moment. "One about a circle and another about a forest, both saying the same thing."

"Neither makes much sense," said Adam.

"Bet they will when Ava talks to me again," said Owen. He walked over to the French doors. "Come on . . . I want to find the Stone Circle. Where does the gate go?"

Holly shrugged. "We've not had time to find out." She led the way up the garden path and looked over the gate. "Owen," she gasped. "The stones! They're right here!"

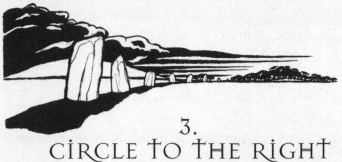

3.
CIRCLE TO THE RIGHT

The tall gray stones marched in a curve along the far side of a daisy-studded field. As Holly, Owen and Adam stared, the sunlight seemed to brighten and shimmer around them.

"They *are* magic stones," breathed Chantel as she hobbled up behind everyone.

Owen unlatched the gate and they entered the field. He stopped and everyone piled into him. He pointed to the sky.

A small hawk circled above. Closer and closer it flew. A feather loosened from its tail and spiraled to the ground as the hawk glided to the top of one of the great stones. It perched and stared haughtily across the field toward them.

"I bet that's Ava. She's sending another message." Owen took off, running toward the fallen feather.

Adam followed.

"Wait for us," Chantel called.

"They never wait," said Holly. She kept pace with Chantel who grasped her crutches and hobbled as fast as she could over the grass.

Owen picked up the feather.

The hawk spread its wings and soared across the deep hollow behind the stones. It disappeared in a distant stand of trees.

Adam touched Owen's shoulder. "Just coincidence. There must be loads of hawks around."

"I suppose so," muttered Owen. He shaded his eyes and strained for a glimpse of the hawk, then tucked the feather in his pocket.

Adam surveyed the nearest megalith. It towered over him. "The stones are humungous. What do you think they weigh?"

Owen's shoulders were hunched with disappointment. He shrugged. "Tons and tons. They're too heavy to move. Ava said the stone turned, but no one could turn these." He leaned against the stone and pushed with all his might.

A strange look came over his face.

Adam wasn't paying attention. He was fooling around the adjacent stone, jumping up to try to touch its topmost edge.

"Here!" Owen's voice was sharp.

"What?" asked Holly as she, Chantel and Adam joined him.

Owen had his hands on the stone. "Feel the stone, and listen," he said.

Everyone placed their palms on the gray surface.

"What are we listening for?" asked Holly.

"Shut up," hissed Owen. "Just do it." He leaned his cheek against the stone and closed his eyes.

Mystified, the other children copied him.

The stone's gritty surface felt surprisingly warm to their cheeks. Each child became aware of sheer bulk, weight and tremendous age. They leaned into the rock and heard and felt a throb, a slow steady pulse beating deep inside.

Everyone's eyes flew open.

"Did you hear it?" said Owen. "Did you?"

"What is it?" asked Chantel.

Owen shook his head, closed his eyes and listened again.

"I know," said Adam quietly. "I've heard it before, in the rocks beneath Wayland's Smithy. It's the heartbeat of the stones. They're alive."

The stones quivered with delight. The children were true shamans. They could hear the stones' hearts. They would listen and learn, and once more the ritual would be performed. Then the stones would be strong again and could fulfill their purpose.

As the stones rejoiced above ground, deep beneath one of them, something stirred.

Trapped in an earthen cell, the night-prowling wraith struggled and writhed. It hated the stones. They were its enemy and jailer. But now the old order was changing.

With each dark came a few hours' freedom. Last night's excursion had been special. Extra strength had filled the night air as if a Dark Power were approaching. A little more dark strength and the wraith could throw off the stones' influence and rise from its cell forever. It already had enough power to meld with an unsuspecting child. The stones would then be powerless to stop it entering the magical center.

They could hurt and imprison the wraith, but they would never hurt a child!

Children were near. Soon . . . soon . . . its time would come. The wraith shrank into a small tight ball to wait.

Holly danced around the stone. "Magic's working. We *are* in the right place."

Adam jabbed her. "People are watching," he said.

They turned to see a group of people laughing at their antics. One of them was a girl in her late teens with plat-form shoes, a black Lycra crop top and dark shiny hair hanging down to the small of her back.

Holly stared admiringly at the girl and immediately became more decorous. She dropped her voice. "I wonder if the other stones have a heartbeat. Let's walk around the Circle and listen."

Owen counted the stones. "There are twelve stones in a curve here, then an enormous gap. A whole bunch are missing." He pointed across the field. "Those big ones in the middle are on their own. They're not part of the Circle. Where are the rest?"

"Follow the ditch," said Holly. "Look." She pointed to the gigantic hollow behind the stones. It curved around and continued after the last standing stone in the line. A path followed the rim. "I bet it goes round in a circle. The stones are set up along the inside rim."

The cousins followed the path, stroking each stone along the way and hearing its heartbeat.

Holly was right. Even when there were missing stones, the ditch continued to circle. Four times there were entrances punched through the ditch, where two roads crossed the

Great Circle. The children crossed the roads. Each time the curve of the ditch continued on the other side, encircling the village, with the stones on guard.

They had almost completed the circuit when the attack happened.

Chantel was lagging behind. It was a long walk on crutches and her leg ached. Ahead of her a hollow in a stone made a seat-like ledge. She sighed with relief. She could rest there.

Chantel limped toward the stone, then paused. She didn't feel good. It was creepy. She felt as though someone was glaring at her, someone who hated her and wished her harm. The hair on the back of her neck prickled. She looked around but saw no one other than her brother and cousins nearby. The nearest people touring the stones were on the other side of the field with their backs to her.

Mystified, Chantel shook her head and started to hobble toward the stone again. Waves of hatred washed over her. She forced her limbs to move. Despite the summer sun, cold sweat trickled down her neck. She swayed with dizziness and drooped over her crutches.

"I mustn't fall," Chantel muttered to herself. "I mustn't. I'll hurt my leg. If only I can make it to the seat." Step by step she forced herself to move closer. The waves of hatred seemed to be coming from the stone itself.

She stopped in confusion. If these were Ava's magic stones they wouldn't hurt her.

"Adam, Holly," she called. "Owen." Her voice was a croak. Sweat beaded her forehead. Blackness gathered behind her eyes. "ADAM!"

Her brother and cousins turned.

"What is it, Chantel?" Holly ran and put her arm around the younger girl. Chantel sagged against her.

Adam ran and supported her other side.

"Get me away from here." With a massive effort, and her brother's and cousin's help, Chantel staggered beyond the stone. As she moved away, the awful feeling lessened. By the time she was leaning against the next stone, she was weak and shaken, but the feeling of hatred was gone.

"What was that all about?" Owen asked.

Chantel shrugged. "I . . . I'm not sure." She tried to explain.

Adam ran back to the stone. He felt nothing. He ran around the stone several times, sat on the ledge and grinned at them. "Goofball, you were imagining it. Too long a walk and too much sun."

Chantel shook her head. "I didn't imagine it. Be careful, Adam Maxwell. There's something nasty near that stone. It might get you."

Adam rolled his eyes.

Once more the wraith lay curled in a ball in its cell. The child had sensed its presence and resisted. It must be sure that didn't happen again.

Now its strength was spent. It must wait. It longed for the velvet darkness of a new night and the growing presence of the unknown power. If all went well it could gather more strength and try again.

"Amazing. The ditch is a perfect circle," said Owen. "And it's big. We must have walked over a mile. But loads of stones are missing. How come?"

"They've fallen down." Holly pointed to one half-buried in the field.

"Some have," said Adam. "But Owen's right. It's more than the odd one falling. Some are gone. I wonder what happened."

"Someone in the museum will know. Let's go there next," Owen said.

"I can't walk any farther," said Chantel.

The others looked at her with concern.

Chantel's face was still pale and she teetered shakily on her crutches.

"She'll never make it home," Holly said. "We should have been helping her instead of galloping ahead."

Adam looked down at his sister. She was small and slight for her age. "I'll piggyback you," he offered.

Owen took the crutches and Adam bent down. Holly boosted Chantel onto Adam's back and he carried her to Manor Cottage.

"We've got to find a better way of getting Chantel around," Owen said as Chantel hopped over to her bed and lay down with a sigh of relief. "We used the pony trap in Uffington." Owen thought for a minute. "We've bikes. Think we could rig up a wagon to pull between us?"

Chantel rolled her eyes. "Yeah, right!" She waved them away. "Go and explore. I'll read." She fiddled in her backpack and brought out a book.

"We'll be back soon," said Owen.

"Better tell Mum where we're going and that Chantel's here," said Holly as they left.

Chantel snuggled into the pillow. Her eyelids drooped and the book slipped from her fingers.

Child, are you there? A gentle voice flowed through her dream.

Is that you, Horse?

A familiar feeling of warmth and friendship washed over Chantel. She smiled in her sleep. Equus, the Great White Horse, had come back to visit her. His mane tickled her cheek and his musky scent of horse sweat and hay surrounded her. *I've missed you,* she murmured.

I've missed you too, Chantel. But you needed time to rest after recovering my talisman. We don't want the burden to become too heavy.

Oh, Horse. Chantel smiled again. *We want to help. It's been hard waiting.*

You are ready for the next task?

Yes, yes. Owen is so excited about Ava's star message, but he doesn't understand what to do.

Tell Owen that Ava will come tonight when he sleeps. Dreams are the easiest way for children to see and understand.

Chantel frowned. *Horse, why don't you just tell us what to do. It's hard to figure things out from dreams.*

Equus laughed, a whinnying bray. *Yes, child, it would save much time. But we cannot undo Human Magic. Humans devised rituals to help them control Earth Magic.*

Humans must perform those rituals. Now do you under-stand?

Sort of, said Chantel doubtfully. *But if you can't do our magic, how come the Dark Being can?*

Equus blew sadly through his nostrils. *She cannot, but she will destroy much before she realizes it.*

There was a long silence.

Horse, said Chantel hesitantly, *let's not talk about the Dark Being anymore. Please, can we go riding?*

Of course. Come, child. I'll show you Ava's Great Cir-cle from the air.

Chantel felt herself rise and there she was, perched on Equus's broad white back. She twisted her hand in his mane and looked down. Manor Cottage and the tiny village of Avebury spread below like a toy model. Around the village ran the deep green ditch and the stones. She gasped. *The Circle is enormous . . . I can see the whole thing from up here.*

Equus gave a whickering chuckle. *It was made that way.*

To be seen from the air? Chantel was puzzled. *Why? I thought it was made a long time ago. Auntie Lynne said five thousand years ago. No one flew then.* She hesitated. *Did they?*

No, said Equus gently. *But we were here. We've always been here.*

Chantel smiled with delight. *The Circle was made for you, like the White Horse carving!*

The Circle was created to honor Ava, the White Horse to honor me.

Chantel stared down while she stroked his neck and

mane. *Not all the stones are in a circle.* Chantel pointed below. *I can see two lines of stones winding over the fields. We didn't notice those from the ground.*

That's the Avenue. It runs from the Circle to the Sanctuary. Equus leaped across the valley to the end of the Avenue. He landed in a field with several rings of concrete blocks in the center. *This is all that's left of the Sanctuary. Markers to show where it once stood.*

What happened? asked Chantel.

Equus shook his great head sadly. *It was destroyed by your people when they discarded Old Magic.*

Chantel gazed downward. She pointed to the conical mound in the distance. *Is Silbury Hill Old Magic too?*

The horse whickered. *It is one of the greatest places of Earth Magic. It is the burial place of King Sel, a great king known for his fairness to his people and for his courage in battle. The mound was built over him where he fell in his last battle. King Sel answers only to himself, but it is said that in times of great danger to Gaia he will ride forth in golden armor on his horse, Aurora, to confront the evil.*

Horse, I want to tell you about something evil. When we walked around the Circle, one of the stones made me feel bad, as though something was looking at me and hating me. It was horrible. Chantel shuddered. *But no one else could feel it.*

I will ask Ava. The stones are not evil, but as our Old Magic strengthens, so does the Dark Magic. Light and Dark, Dark and Light. Ava will know what hides near her stones. Until we know what the evil is, tell the others to stay away.

I will. But why was it only me that felt it?

You are the Magic Child. You worked with me and are more aware and sensitive to enchantment. As the other children work with us, their senses will expand too.

Holly can sense things. An oak tree talked to her when we were in the forest.

Chantel felt Equus stiffen. *One of the sacred oaks?*

I think so. Holly said it was the Mother Tree.

What wonderful news you bring me, Chantel. Thank you. Let us ride the wind and celebrate!

Chantel leaned forward as Equus leaped for the stars. They galloped along sunbeams, cantered through clouds of stardust and jumped over galaxies. The winds of time lifted Chantel's curls and whispered wordless songs in her ears. Finally she drooped with exhaustion over Equus's neck.

Sleep and dream, child. Sleep and dream. Call if you need me. I will not be far away.

The voice faded. Chantel slept.

She woke with a start. A squeaking sound and chuckles were coming from the patio. She leaned up on one elbow and stared.

A giant wicker basket on wheels stood outside the French doors.

Holly poked her head into the bedroom. "Good, you're awake. See what we found in the antique shop across the road." She giggled again. "It's called a Bath chair. We've talked the owner, Mrs. Bates, into renting it for the week."

Chantel burst out laughing. "A *bath* chair! It won't hold much water!"

"That's what I said," chuckled Owen. "But Mrs. Bates said they were first made in the city of Bath."

The Bath chair was really an old-fashioned wheelchair made of woven cane. Crimson leather cushions padded the seat, and the wicker webbing rose over it in a hood. It had three wheels. Two large wheels with rubber tires supported the back. A metal handle rose from the chassis and curved up around the hood. A smaller wheel in the middle of the long leg rest at the front had a shaft and steering mechanism for the occupant to guide it.

"Go on, sit in it. We push, you steer." Owen chuckled. "But watch it. The hood is so big we can't see where we're going."

Chantel hopped over and wiggled in. There was lots of room for her cast to stretch out comfortably. She grasped the steering bar. Owen and Adam leaned on the handle.

Despite squeaks, the Bath chair moved smoothly forward.

Owen and Adam pushed and Chantel steered down the path, along the side of the house and across the gravel courtyard. They paused at the road. It was empty. They bowled out into the street.

"Faster!" called Chantel.

The boys grinned at each other and started to jog.

Passersby stared and someone whistled.

The boys propelled the Bath chair at a spanking pace down the street. A hedge rose in front of them. Chantel suddenly realized that the road came to a dead end. At the last minute she turned the front wheel and they swung round the next corner. A teenage girl holding an ice cream appeared in front of them.

"STOP!" yelled Chantel.

Adam dug in his heels and Owen yanked on the brake. The Bath chair screeched to a halt, but not before the leg rest bumped into the back of the teenager's knee and knocked her off balance.

"Idiots!" the girl shouted, her arms flailing above her head in an effort to stay upright. The ice cream shot from the cone, flew through the air and landed in her hair.

Owen and Adam muffled snorts of laughter. Chantel tried not to chuckle.

Holly cycled up behind them. "Oops," she said with a laugh.

Then she saw that the victim was the dark-haired teen she had admired earlier. "We're so sorry," she said. "We were trying out the Bath chair so our cousin doesn't have to walk everywhere with her broken leg." Holly babbled on and on in an attempt to smooth things over. "Here." She fished into her jeans pocket and brought out some change. "We'll buy you another ice cream. We're really, really sorry."

The girl ignored Holly and glared at Chantel and the boys. "Just watch it in future," she said icily, wiping the mess off her long dark hair with a tissue. She stalked past them.

Holly flushed.

Adam struggled to control himself but made the mistake of looking at Chantel.

"Bad hair day," Chantel said.

All three cousins howled with laughter.

"You are *so* embarrassing," said Holly. She turned her bike and cycled away.

"We're in this village for ten minutes, and already I'm hearing stories of the mad Maxwell kids," grumbled Uncle Ron at teatime. "As for that contraption outside, how long do you kids think it will last if you crash into people? You won't be renting it for a week. You'll be paying for it out of your pocket money for years to come. You realize it's an antique?"

"You could have hurt someone," said Aunt Lynne.

"We'll be careful now we know how fast it can go. It's brilliant though, isn't it, Dad?" said Owen.

"Out!" Owen's father pointed to the patio. "You know the deal. You're not eating inside with us until you find a washing machine."

"I thought you were joking," Owen protested.

"The joke's on you, son. You can join us when you smell better."

Owen grabbed his plate and stomped into the kitchen.

Adam and Chantel exchanged glances, sank down in their chairs and got on with their spaghetti.

"Actually, the Bath chair was a brilliant idea," Uncle Ron said, grinning across at Chantel. "As long as you don't mind riding in it."

Chantel gave a shy smile and shook her head.

"I'll pay for the rental. Holly, come and settle up with me after tea. Just treat the darn chair with respect. It belonged to Lady Mayerthorpe at the manor. People around here remember her using it."

Adam gave a snort and jabbed Chantel in the ribs. "Don't get any ideas about being Lady Whatshername," he whispered.

"Thanks, Dad," said Holly. "Where is the manor? Is it

nearby? Is that why this place is called Manor Cottage?"

"I thought you explored the village this afternoon."

Holly grinned. "We went round the stones, but other than the chariot race we never got past the antique shop across the road."

Her father laughed. He pulled several tourist brochures out of his pocket. "I picked up these. One's a map of the village." He spread it out on the table and jabbed his finger in the middle. "We're right in the center of the Circle. The barns next door are the museum complex. Here's the manor, behind the church at the end of the road. It's also part of the museum complex. The family still lives there, but you can go around the gardens and I think the ground floor of the house is open to the public." He pushed the other folders across to Holly, then took out his wallet and extracted four plastic tags. "Look after these. They will get you into the museums and the manor as many times as you like, without paying."

"Dad, you're the greatest." Holly ran around the table and gave him a hug.

"We can get in the museum free? Great! We can find out more about the Stone Circle," Owen said as he bounded back into the dining room dressed only in a towel clutched around his waist.

"I see you've discovered the washing machine." Lynne chuckled. She eyed the towel. "Does this mean you brought *only* dirty clothes?"

"That's no problem. They'll be clean soon." Owen was unrepentant. "There's a dryer too." He grinned at his mother. "Do you have any washing you'd like me to pop in?"

His mum laughed and made a mock attempt to tweak away his towel.

With a yell, Owen ran back into the kitchen.

Adam and Chantel watched the family byplay.

"I wish our mom and dad teased and laughed," whispered Adam.

"Me too," agreed Chantel.

They lapsed into unhappy silence.

The hawk flew out of the trees and circled high over the stones, watching and waiting.

As the sun set, the summer twilight freed the shadows. They lengthened and stretched, hiding where stone finished and ground began. The hawk circled watchfully, for as the shadows gathered, the beings of the night stirred.

This night nothing seemed amiss. A steady stream of bats flew above the Circle, weaving, darting and snatching at insects. They spotted the hawk and circled it in acknowledgment, then returned to their feeding.

The night-prowling wraith emerged.

The hawk stared down.

The wraith prowled around the Circle, searching for the entrance it was always denied. Though its mist seemed stronger and denser, its actions were the same as always. There was nothing to suggest it knew that the Dark Power was approaching.

The hawk relaxed. The wraith had been no threat for hundreds of years. Reassured, she glided to the roof of Manor Cottage, folded her wings and waited for sleep to overtake the chosen child.

4.
CIRCLE MAGIC

"Adam, Adam, are you asleep?" whispered Owen.

It was midnight and they'd been talking for ages, but Adam had fallen quiet in midsentence.

Owen tossed and turned. He was so eager for Ava to contact him that sleep was impossible. He couldn't believe his luck. He was the one the Wise Ones were talking to, not his Canadian cousins and not his older sister. He sat up and pulled back the curtain.

"Come on, Ava," he whispered. "Where are you?" He pictured her as he had last seen her in the Place Beyond Morning, an imposing half-woman, half-bird, whose beauty made his breath catch. He stared at the stars, willing her to come, until his eyes watered. Eventually sleep won. Owen sprawled back on his pillow, one foot thrust out of the sheets, snoring gently.

The image of a hawk circled through his dreams. She flew closer and closer.

Come, fly with me, Owen. Ava's voice filled his mind.

In his dream, Owen spread his arms and soared into the air through the open window. "Brilliant!" he laughed. He flew a wobbly course down the road between the darkened houses and experimented, banking one way, then swiftly turning the other. It was wonderful! He had never experienced such freedom. He flapped his arms furiously, tucked in his head and turned a couple of shaky somersaults. Somehow he managed to level out before hitting the ground. "Fan-bloody-tastic!" he shouted. He looked around and saw the hawk hovering above him.

Don't shout, she reproved him. *It hurts my head. Mindspeak. I'll hear you.*

Where are we going? Owen asked as he flew clumsily up to join Ava.

Into the past, replied Ava. *But first I have much to explain. Come.* She glided to the church tower and perched on one arm of the weather vane.

Flapping frantically, legs making ungainly swimming motions, Owen followed and crash-landed on the roof.

Ouch! This takes a bit of practice. He rubbed a bruised knee and sat on the edge of the tower battlements, feet dangling.

It was a magnificent night. Below them spread the sleeping village. No lights showed, nothing stirred. Above them spread the star-studded midnight sky and a moon so bright it threw everything into sharp relief. The landscape was crisscrossed with silver light and blue shadows.

The stones dominated. They stood, silvered sentinels, forever on guard.

Owen sat, drinking it all in.

What do you see? said Ava.

Owen waved his arm, almost lost for words. *The stones, the village, the sky. It's beautiful.*

Look again . . . Do you see any veils of darkness?

Owen scanned the landscape. *Like what?*

Ava was silent.

Owen looked again. *Only . . .* He hesitated *. . . . a bit of mist rising near one of the stones . . . and . . .* He shrugged. *. . . a blank bit of sky . . . as though a small cloud is covering the stars.* He pointed toward the vast sweep of the Milky Way.

Well done, child, Ava said. *You know how to observe. Always watch for mist or cloud when all else is clear. What seems like a cloud in the sky is small but important. It is blackness obscuring the approach of the Dark Being. She has entered your universe and is searching each star for our tools. So far Gaia has escaped her attention, but the Wise Ones must regain their tools before she discovers your planet and takes them for herself.*

Ava turned her head and gazed at the Circle.

The mist near my stones is an elemental, a night-prowling wraith. The stones have it under control. They confine it by day, and it prowls around the outside edge of the Circle at night. It is an unwitting servant of the Dark Being, though it knows nothing of her. As the Dark Being approaches, it gains strength. So will other elementals, both of darkness and light, lurking on this place you call Earth. As our Old Magic rises, so does the Dark Magic. Light and dark must balance for harmony. There cannot be one without the other, but one must not overpower the other or both magics will be destroyed.

Why does the Dark Being want your tools? asked Owen.

It doesn't make sense if upsetting the balance destroys things.

Ava sighed. *Power sometimes corrupts the mind. She is so hungry for more power that she has stopped believing in the balance.*

So we are going to be destroyed? Owen shuddered. *Everyone on earth is going to be killed?*

Ava flew down and perched on the battlement beside him. *Child, listen. It is our power that will be destroyed. Then both the Dark Being and the Wise Ones will be nothing.* She touched his arm with her wing. *We wish to avoid trouble by finding the tools and removing them from Gaia. Then you will never be troubled by her.*

Owen frowned. *But . . . but what if she gets you? What about the balance? You said there must always be dark and light. What happens if you are nothing?*

Ava was silent for a long time. *I do not know, for we have always been,* she admitted finally. *But Gaia will change.*

Owen stared at the landscape beneath him. This was heavy-duty stuff. It had seemed such fun when they had entered into the first adventure, but now that he had seen the cloud, evil hung in the air. Unthinkingly, he put out his hand and stroked the hawk beside him, drawing comfort from her warmth and softness.

He stilled his hand and turned to look at her. Ava was a hawk now, but the image of her beauty as a Wise One filled his mind.

He snatched back his hand. *I'm sorry . . . I didn't mean to be rude.*

I didn't feel rudeness, only affection and a need for reassurance, said Ava. She answered his unspoken question. *Yes,*

I am a shape-changer. Humans are more comfortable with shapes they recognize, so when on Gaia with you, I am a hawk or a woman. Tonight we fly, so I am a hawk.

What must I do to help? asked Owen quietly.

You must watch the past, then gather the main elements of your earth's Old Magic and use them to unlock the secret of the stones. This will release my circlet. Ava shook out her feathers, stretched and flexed her wings. *It is time to fly, child. Follow me.* She flew off the tower and headed toward the Stone Circle.

Owen gulped. The ground was a long way down. He had flown out of the window on impulse, but now he had to launch himself off a high tower. In the first flush of the magic he had forgotten how much he hated heights.

A feeling of strength and safety flooded over him. *You are my chosen helper, Owen. Another Magic Child like Chantel. You will not fall.*

Owen closed his eyes, gathered his courage and tried to jump into space. He couldn't move.

Owen, do you trust me?

Er . . . yes. Owen's voice shook. He tried to block out a vision of his body smashing into the ground.

Believe in the magic and believe in yourself. You can fly.

Ava swooped down and pushed Owen in the middle of his back.

He tumbled off the tower yelling, kicking and flapping frantically.

The air streamed past him, but there was no sense of the ground coming up to meet him. Owen opened one eye.

He was high above the earth. "Thanks, Ava," he yelled, forgetting to mindspeak in his astonishment. He followed her.

Below them, the stones surrounded the dreaming village. Ava began to trace their circle.

Owen tucked in behind her. He flapped when Ava flapped and glided when she glided. They flew faster. The Circle below seemed to turn, or was it them? The midnight sky whirled and the wind rushed past him, flattening his feathers . . . HIS FEATHERS? Owen was a boy no more. His feet were talons. His arms were wings. His nose was a beak. He was a hawk.

Their speed increased. Round and round they circled. Night and day blurred as they hurtled through countless sunrises and sunsets, until Ava's wingbeats slowed.

Owen gasped. A snowflake landed on his beak and a chilly winter wind buffeted him. They were wheeling high above the Avebury Circle, but gone were the village and the surrounding fields and downs. The land below was forested, an enormous oak forest that flowed over hills and valleys as far as he could see.

Small gaps showed in the forest. Occasionally the top of a hill was cleared and a simple village of huts, surrounded by a protective fence, huddled on the summit. Several hunting trails could be seen, and a dry streambed, but the biggest clearing held the Stone Circle.

The Great Circle was magnificent, covered in snow.

The ditch surrounding it was twice as deep as the modern one. The high embankment that Owen had walked gleamed white against the dark forest. It dipped in four places to create four imposing entrances, one for each direction. From two entrances, pairs of stones marched through the forest in wide cleared avenues. One ended suddenly, but the other avenue marched for over a mile, linking the Great Circle to a tiny stone circle on a far hill. That circle contained a small round hut.

Most striking of all were the features within the Great Circle. For it was not one circle, but three. Two smaller circles stood side by side within the gigantic outer circle. The outer circle was not quite complete. A dark hole yawned in a gap where one stone was missing.

Owen struggled to make sense of all he saw.

You are looking at the past, said Ava. *Observe silently. We are seeing my Circle as it was four thousand years ago. You cannot be part of its history. You can only be part of its future. A past ritual magically hid my circlet forever. Observe the ritual carefully for clues. Your task is to create a future ritual that will release it.*

I don't get it. Owen was puzzled. *If you can see into the past, you must know where your circlet is. Why don't you fetch it?*

Only the people of Gaia can open their sacred places without disrupting the balance. It must be done freely. Because of your offer to help, you four children have become the representatives of Gaia.

What if we mess up? Owen replied worriedly.

Ava did not reply.

They spiraled downward.

Owen's hawk eyes spotted movements far below. Ant-like dots were converging on the Great Circle.

As they flew closer, the ants became humans wearing

woolen tunics, wraps and skin capes.

A group of seven people, in a solemn procession, were walking from the hut in the distant circle along the main avenue of stones.

Making their way along the second avenue were over a hundred people hauling a massive stone over a frozen trail toward the Great Circle.

A small group of men were working around the gap in the Great Circle.

A large crowd was gathering along the massive embankment to watch.

Ava and Owen circled lower. Ava swooped and landed on a standing stone. She folded her wings, puffed up her feathers to keep warm and watched the past with bright hawk eyes.

Now you must concentrate, child. Ava's voice filled Owen's mind. *See the past through the eyes of Hewll, the Pit Maker.* Ava fixed her hawk gaze on a young man laboring at the edge of the large hole.

Owen did the same.

5.
THE FINAL STONE

The morning was cold with a swirl of light snow. Despite the frigid temperature, Hewll brushed away beads of sweat. He grasped his antler pick and urged his team of Pit Makers to finish the ramp into the last pit.

The final stone was almost there.

The People of the Hawk and the People of the Deer shouted encouragement from the embankment around the great ditch.

Hewll ran his eyes over his tribe. No one was missing, not even Old One Eye, who could barely walk. Hewll gave a nod of approval. No one should miss this sight. This was the day foretold by the tribe's grandparents' grandparents' grandparents' grandparent. This was the day of completion. The wondrous day the great Stone Circle would finally reflect the eternal circles of Ava, the hawk-mother who watched over them and carried their spirits to the sky.

A shout made him turn. "The Maidens are here!"

"Enough!" Hewll motioned his team out of the hole.

Young girls carrying skin buckets full of water appeared. They crossed the snow-covered ground, dripping water that instantly formed a slick of ice. They trickled water over the ramp. It glazed the slope.

Hewll smiled. Ulwin was the second maiden. There was no mistaking her lithe figure, despite the heavy wool wrap she had swathed around her head and body against the bitter cold. After the work was completed, he and Ulwin would be bonded at the feast.

She flashed him a grin as she passed.

Hewll swelled with pride.

Psst, Ava, said Owen to the hawk on the stone beside him. A movement had broken his concentration, a gathering of mist swirling at the base of the stone beside him. *That misty thing. Is it the night-prowling wraith? Is it the same thing you showed me from the church?*

Yes, Ava replied. *The wraith was here before the stones. There have been elementals on Gaia as long as there have been people.*

But it's daylight.

In the beginning the wraith roamed freely, though it preferred night. Only after it tried to disrupt the power of the Circle did the stones subdue it and limit its movements. Concentrate, Owen. Watch.

Owen turned back to his task, slipping again into Hewll's mind.

Hewll heard the thump of the logs and the panting, grunting and cursing of men. The Rollers and Pullers were near.

A sudden shout of welcome erupted. The tribes' two shamans and their five apprentices had completed the sacred Walk of Seven along the Avenue from the Sanctuary. They stepped through the Shaman's Entrance into the Great Circle.

Hewll gasped. The chief shaman's upper face was concealed by a golden half-mask resembling a hawk's eyes and beak. A woven helmet threaded with dancing, fluttering hawk feathers completed the illusion. Her eyes glittered behind the holes. A gleaming gold-handled sickle was tucked into her belt and a gilded horn was slung on a cord over her shoulder. Behind her walked an apprentice bearing a mistletoe bough.

The second shaman followed wearing a deer-like leather half-mask and a massive crown of intertwined deer antlers. He carried a small clay pot. Two men and two women followed chanting, "Fare to the Stones. Fare to the Circle."

"Peace is within. Leave behind evil," Hewll and the tribes' people answered.

The chief shaman stood beside the pit and drew forth her sickle. "Blessed be the sacred mistletoe," she intoned, "whose roots need no earth and drink no water, whose dried remains are used to light the sacred fire and whose juices protect us from dark spirits."

"Blessed be the mistletoe," replied the tribes' people.

Gold flashed as the chief shaman severed the mistletoe ball from the bough and cast it into the pit.

The second shaman entered the smaller of the inner circles. Pulling two flints from his pocket he shouted, "Behold, the fire stones! Spitters of flame, lighters of darkness, givers of warmth, shield against our enemies."

"Blessed be the fire stones," the tribes' people cried.

Hewll held his breath as the second shaman smashed the stones together.

A spark flashed and a tiny ember smoldered. The shaman blew. A flame greedily licked dried flakes of mistletoe and began to consume them.

"The fire, the fire, blessed be the sacred fire," roared Hewll and the tribes' people.

Soon a great bonfire roared.

The chief shaman lifted the horn from her shoulder and blew. "Behold, the last Sarsen Stone," she called in a high clear voice.

THUD! A log dropped across the Moon Entrance. Men grasping braided ropes leaped over the log, straining and pulling to keep the tension on the lines. The gray end of the Sarsen edged slowly into the Circle.

Hewll crossed his fingers and spat, making the ancient charm for luck, as inch by inch the stone moved forward.

The Rollers and Pullers worked in teams, carrying logs from behind to be laid once more before the stone. The logs rolled on the ground and eased the stone forward. Men took over from men, keeping the massive ropes taut and another log ready. The slow steady momentum must not stop. Those at the front grunted, strained and pulled. Those at the back pushed and coaxed with heavy wooden levers.

The onlookers cheered them on.

The stone edged across the Circle toward the hole.

The fire blazed in celebration.

"All that remains now is the perfect drop," whispered Hewll to his neighbor.

The Sarsen teetered over the pit, then shook the ground as it fell on the icy ramp and plunged down to bury its end perfectly in the center, crushing the mistletoe.

Hewll yelled with delight. He turned to the Pit Makers and they slapped each other on the back.

The dance changed.

Ropes were harnessed to the top of the stone. The Pit Makers, Rollers and Pullers joined forces to gather up the logs and thrust and brace them beneath the angle of the stone. Hewll threw himself into the work using a large wooden lever.

Inch by inch the stone moved upright.

The sun began its descent.

Women brought more fuel. Soon the fire blazed brighter than the setting sun.

Shadows lengthened and still the people toiled.

At last the shaman's horn blew.

The stone stood.

Once more an uneasy feeling distracted Owen. He drew back into his hawk body and looked again at the stone beside him. The mist at its base bubbled and boiled.

Ava, what's happening to the wraith? It seems angry.

Ava sighed. *It is angry. It wants to disrupt the ceremony and destroy my power.*

Can it do that? asked Owen anxiously.

It will try.

Hewll rose and leaped into action. "Dig," he yelled.

Grasping white bone shovels made from oxen scapula, he and his team began to refill the pit. They worked long into the winter night. Finally the stone stood firm. The Circle was complete.

Hewll and the Pit Makers stood together on the rim of the gigantic ditch. "Rejoice!" shouted Hewll. "Our picks and shovels have raised a sacred stone; any lesser job would defile them. Let them keep their memory of triumph. Tomorrow we will hunt an ox and deer and make new ones."

"AYE!" shouted his fellow workers. They tossed their antler picks and bone shovels high in the air. The tools turned, catching gleams of firelight before falling into the darkness of the ditch.

Men, women and children rushed between the stones and held hands to make their own circle — a circle inside a circle. The horn blew, the shamans chanted and the people lifted their voices and sang.

Light and Dark, Dark and Light,
Sun by day, Moon by night . . .

Hewll grasped Ulwin's hand and they joined a dance that wound between the stones. The song quickened. The dancers moved faster. They whirled and swirled until, "The stones, they dance with us," Ulwin cried.

The horn sounded again.

The dancers reeled dizzily to a stop. Silence fell.

The chief shaman pulled a leather bag from inside her tunic and held its treasured contents aloft.

A small circlet of twisted silver strands glinted in the

firelight. A white stone embedded in the front glowed like the moon.

The people fell to their knees.

"Since time uncounted we have protected Ava's circlet," shouted the chief shaman. "But look your last, People of the Hawk. Look your last, People of the Deer. Tell your grandchildren, so they can tell their children's grandchildren, of the day we passed our treasure to the Sarsen Stones. Their memories are as long as Earth herself. Wind will not fell them, rain will not wear them, sun will not burn them and the moon will watch over them. When the People of the Hawk and Deer are gone, the Sarsens will stand to protect Ava's circlet forever."

The chief shaman motioned for Hewll to step forward.

The second shaman reached for an antler from his crown and handed it to Hewll.

They walked into the second small circle. The shamans lit a ring of brands, then pointed to a spot on the ground in the center. Hewll knelt and with the antler's tip scraped away loosened dirt. He exposed a flat rock and pried it up. A small slab-lined cavity was revealed.

The chief shaman held the circlet up to the moon and murmured a blessing.

Hewll trembled in awe, his eyes riveted on the circlet. He sighed as the chief shaman dropped it in the skin bag. She placed the bag inside the small pot held out by the second shaman, and he placed the pot in the cavity.

"Who bringeth the water?" asked the chief shaman.

An apprentice lifted a small gourd that hung from a cord around her throat.

"Blessed be the water from the stream that doesn't run, for it giveth life," murmured the watching tribes' people.

The chief shaman plucked a feather from her helmet, dipped it in the gourd and shook droplets over the cavity.

Hewll replaced the slab.

Both shamans sprinkled a handful of earth over it, then Hewll refilled the hole and stomped on the ground to firm it.

Again the chief shaman dipped her feather in the flask and sprinkled water.

Hewll gasped. As the drops hit the ground, grass grew and hid the scar in the earth.

"You all bear witness," chorused the shamans, their voices breaking the silence.

"We all bear witness," replied everyone softly.

"Reveal and die."

"Reveal and die," the people promised.

The tribes' people held hands and made a circle, a human circle around the small stone circle.

"Let the Circle keep its secret while stones stand and hawks fly," everyone shouted, then chanted, "Ava, Ava, AVA, AVA."

Hewll pointed in amazement. He'd spotted two watching hawks.

The largest bird spread her wings, left her stone and circled above them.

"AVA! AVA! AVA! AVA!" the people roared as the hawk's black shape appeared against the moon and circled above them before disappearing into the night.

Owen shifted uneasily in his hawk's body. His concentration had broken when Ava left his side. He was tired and cold and could no longer see with Hewll's eyes. He ruffled his feathers, moved his feet and wished that Ava would return.

The cold seeped into his bones. Gradually Owen realized that this wasn't just cold from the weather, but a deadly cold coming from the mist at the base of the next stone. He peered down.

A wild boar had left the forest and was snuffling for mushrooms near the Circle. The wraith enfolded its mist around the boar and disappeared — absorbed into the boar's body.

Instantly, the boar's eyes gleamed red. It snorted angrily.

Owen watched in horror as the boar charged between the stones. With his last remnants of strength, he reached out to Hewll one more time.

A sense of foreboding filled Hewll. He stared around the Circle, but nothing seemed amiss. All was quiet for the final blessing.

Then a terrible snorting erupted as a wild boar, tusks glinting wickedly in the firelight, entered the Circle. Its angry eyes searched for a victim.

Children screamed and hid behind stones. Women gathered up infants and dragged back the elders.

The chief shaman turned. Her glittering mask attracted the boar. It charged.

A fleeing figure stumbled and fell. The boar gored her leg. Ulwin screamed and twisted to keep her belly from the pointed tusks.

Hewll ran to the fire, pulled out a burning brand and thrust it into the boar's face.

"Crawl away," he yelled to Ulwin.

"I can't," she shrieked. "Its tusk is caught in my cloak."

Squealing with terror and anger the boar tried to retreat. Its cloven hooves trampled Ulwin. She screamed again.

Hewll jammed the blazing brand into the boar's eye and tugged at Ulwin's cloak. The hunters were closing in to help, but no one wanted to loose a spear while the girl was entangled.

"A knife," called Hewll. A tusk grazed his arm. He thrust the burning brand forward again.

The shaman threw her sickle and Hewll sawed at the twist of cloth. It parted and he staggered backward, pulling Ulwin with him.

The hunters rushed forward. They skewered the boar in the neck and belly and yanked it up on its hind feet. The chief shaman retrieved her sickle and slashed the boar's throat.

Ulwin's weak cry of triumph was echoed by the crowd.

Owen could stay inside Hewll no more. He huddled, retching, on the stone, and watched the faint wraith mist rise from the dead boar's mouth.

Unseen by the tribes' people, the stone beside Owen quivered. The earth at its base yawned open. The stone spun quickly on its axis, creating a vortex, a whirlpool in the ground. With a silent cry of pain and defeat, the wraith was sucked beneath the earth. The hole closed. The wraith was banished.

A shout drew Owen's attention again to the Circle. The

hunters had removed the boar's head and were stripping meat from its bones.

Children rushed forward and grabbed the head. They tossed it one to the other and paraded it around the Circle for all to see.

"Stuff its wicked mouth," shouted Old One Eye. "Show it ain't going to worrit and terrorize us no more." He threw a dried apple to the children. Laughing, they wedged it between the teeth. The children paraded the head again as the crowd hooted with glee.

Sickened by the scene, Owen barely noticed the snow falling or the icy wind growing in strength until he was finally blown off his stone. Snowflakes swirled around him. The people blurred, the firelight vanished, the stones disappeared. The roaring blizzard tossed Owen like a feather in the wind.

HELP . . . AVA!

Fly, Owen.

I can't.

You can, I'm here; I'm always here.

Strength flooded Owen's body. He flapped his wings and beat by beat rose above the storm. Far below was a whirlpool of white flakes, but here the night sky was clear, the stars bright. Beside him was Ava.

Side by side they circled. Faster and faster they flew. The universe whirled.

You've taken a long journey, Owen, said Ava. *Thank you. Now you can rest.*

Owen closed his eyes and spiraled down into the comforting velvet blackness of sleep.

6.
SWING YOUR PARTNERS

"Ava, Myrddin, I am uneasy." Equus pawed the sky restlessly. "Chantel has sensed an evil presence near Ava's stones."

"The wraith is gaining strength again," said Ava.

"Gaia's elementals are stirring," rumbled Myrddin. "More will stir the closer the Dark Being gets. How close is she, Equus?"

"The shadow falls across at least a quarter of the Milky Way."

"Do the humans not see it?" asked Myrddin.

"They see only clouds." Equus sighed. "Maybe it is better that way."

"No . . . they are unprepared." Ava's voice was sharper than usual. "If they understood, they could try to conquer the despair and hate the Dark Being brings. Instead they will never know why suddenly they are fighting one another."

"Do the children know they may be attacked?" asked Myrddin.

"I have warned Owen about the Dark Being, but told him we will protect Gaia by letting her claim the tools," Ava said unhappily.

"And so we shall, though at dreadful cost." Myrddin sighed. "The earthly elementals must be carefully watched. Though many will keep the balance, some make much trouble."

Ava drew herself up and spread her wings. Her fierce beauty shone. "You are right, Myrddin. I must warn Owen that they may have to do battle with the wraith. The stones have subdued it for so many centuries that I had discounted it, but the wraith could be dangerous as it gains strength. I showed it to Owen, but I will explain further."

"I have hopeful news," said Equus. "The oldest child, Holly, senses Old Magic. The Mother Tree has spoken to her."

Myrddin's face showed his relief. "The new dawn has stirred more than Ava's stones. The supporters of light are rallying." His lips parted in a rare smile. "So the oldest child heard the Mother Tree without our help. Well, well, well! I have great hopes for her."

Equus shifted uneasily. "She is too young."

"So was Adam. Yet when searching for your talisman, he was tempted by the dragon and resisted. He found his own strength," said Myrddin.

Equus sighed. "We too must strengthen our defenses for battle. Concealment is not enough. We must seek knowledge of the Dark Being's movements. I will ride the wind to the edge of the shadow."

"Be careful, Equus." Ava touched his back with a wing.

"I regret that you must go alone, but without our tools Myrddin and I are powerless to travel with you."

"Travel only among sunbeams," advised Myrddin. "The Dark Being abhors the sun."

"Going alone will be less dangerous," replied Equus. "It will be easier to escape detection, and the talisman can protect me." He bunched his hind muscles in preparation. The gold disk on his forelock gleamed as he leaped across the sky and disappeared in a swirl of stardust.

Myrddin stamped his foot. "Oh, for my staff! I cannot abide this feeling of helplessness."

"Faith, Myrddin. We will all regain our tools and the Lady will rise again. Traa dy liooar, remember?"

"Yes, yes. Traa dy liooar . . . we hope!" echoed Myrddin in a voice of deep foreboding.

"So!" Adam said as Owen finally woke.

"So, what?" Owen yawned sleepily.

"So, did Ava come?"

"And how." Owen's face lit up. He stretched out his arms and looked at them in wonder. "She turned me into a hawk and we flew into the past." He rolled out of bed. "Come on. Let's wake the girls and I'll tell you about it."

Adam thumped his pillow and followed, slamming the door in fury. He couldn't believe Ava had chosen Owen over him. It wasn't fair.

It was still well before breakfast time when the boys converged on the girls' bedroom and Owen recounted his night's adventure.

Adam listened but fidgeted as frustration built inside him. This adventure was supposed to be his.

"The boar sounds awful," said Chantel, shuddering, her eyes as big as saucers. "Were you scared?"

"Sort of." Owen wrinkled his nose. "The way they killed it was gross. I thought I'd throw up when the kids started chucking its head around."

"So Ava said we are supposed to get things and reenact some kind of ritual?" asked Adam.

Owen nodded.

"Well if that means cutting the throat of a boar, count me out!" Adam's voice was full of disgust.

Chantel went white. She shook her head furiously. "No . . . no, that's not right . . . Equus and the others . . . they wouldn't . . . " Her voice trailed off.

"Shut up, Adam. You're scaring Chantel," Holly said.

Owen patted Chantel's arm. "Of course we won't have to kill anything. That was thousands of years ago." He turned back to Adam. "Ava was just showing me what happened when the Circle was completed. We don't have to kill animals. I think we just need to gather some of the things they used in the ceremony."

"I don't get it," said Adam. "How will that help? If Ava's circlet is buried somewhere in the center of the Circle, in another circle that's disappeared, we still don't know where to dig."

Owen looked worried. "I know." He gestured beyond the end of the garden. "Nothing out there looks like the place I saw in my dream. Stones are missing. The village is in the middle. A road is cutting across. There's no forest." He spread his hands helplessly. "I don't recognize anything."

"Hold on," said Holly. "We're dealing with magic. We might not have to know where it's buried. You said something about . . . gathering elements of magic . . . and . . . and using them to release the circlet."

Owen nodded excitedly. "You're right. Ava said. 'This will release my circlet.' So maybe we don't have to dig. Maybe, if we use the right magic, the circlet appears on its own." He paused, looking thoughtful. "Do you think the mistletoe is an element?"

"I can get you that!" Holly said. She jabbed Owen's ribs. "You laughed when I told you the Mother Tree had offered me mistletoe. Go on, eat your words!"

Owen grinned. "Watch it, Clever Clogs, or your hat won't fit."

"What about the fire?" asked Chantel hesitantly. "That seemed important too."

"Easy!" said Adam sarcastically. "We'll light a big bonfire in the Circle and invite the whole village." He smirked at Owen. "I suppose you're going to dance round it?"

"'The time is near for the Circle Dance,'" quoted Holly softly. "Someone has to dance."

"Yeah right," Adam snorted. "Then there's the water . . . I suppose that's something we have to use?"

Owen opened his mouth to reply, but Adam rushed on. "Yup, we'll take a pail and fling water around and tell everyone we're blessing the stones." Adam snorted. "Rituals, smituals!" He stood up. "I'm going for breakfast."

Owen grabbed Chantel's hairbrush and pitched it after him.

"What's eating Adam?" asked Holly as he left the room.

"He's mad because Ava's chosen me instead of him," muttered Owen.

"He's often mad," said Chantel sadly. "But it used to be all the time and just at me." She grinned suddenly. "Now he gets mad at you and leaves me alone."

Owen threw a pillow at her. "Thanks a lot."

Holly jumped off her bed and stretched. "Forget Adam. Do you think we've guessed some of the elements, Owen? Mistletoe, fire and water. That makes three."

Owen nodded. "I think so."

"Is that it, or do we need to figure out more?" said Chantel.

Owen shrugged. "Dunno." He looked at Holly. "How will you get to the forest for mistletoe?"

"I'll think of something. Maybe we can persuade Mum to take us for a picnic."

Owen moved over to sit beside Chantel. "What should we do about Adam?"

Chantel pulled her face. "Leave him. He'll come round."

"He makes me feel guilty." Owen sounded frustrated. "He really expected to be chosen this time."

Chantel wriggled uncomfortably. She tried to choose words that didn't sound disloyal. "He always feels left out. Then he gets mad." She raised her eyes to Owen. "He didn't use to be mad all the time. He played with me lots when I was little . . . it's just been this last year . . . since Mom and Dad . . . " Chantel's voice faded away. "It's not your fault," she finished.

"They're your parents too. How come you're not mad all the time?" asked Owen.

"I don't think about it," Chantel said simply. "When things get bad, I kind of go away in my head and make up stories."

Holly chuckled. "Adam told us you lived in an imaginary world. He was right." She came over and hugged the younger girl. "Because of your imagination you weren't surprised to hear the Wise Ones." She looked thoughtful. "We'd better think of a way of distracting Adam." She walked over to the dressing table and held up the four plastic tickets her dad had produced the night before. "Let's visit the museum. He'll like that. Maybe he'll discover some information to help us find other magical elements."

Adam stomped downstairs, sick with disappointment. It wasn't fair. The Wise Ones were ignoring him. He wanted to fly with Ava or ride with Equus in his dreams, but first it had been his nerdy little sister and now Owen. When was it going to be his turn? He deserved it. He had given Equus the talisman when he could have kept it for himself. Maybe that was what he should have done . . . kept it. Then he would have power over the whole world and the Wise Ones would have to talk to him. He sighed. He was so sick of being a ten-year-old kid no one cared about.

Uncle Ron was reading the newspaper, and Adam was munching toast when the rest of the kids gathered at the breakfast table.

Uncle Ron flipped down the corner of the paper and smiled at them. "Good morning."

"Morning, Dad," chorused Holly and Owen. Chantel smiled shyly.

Owen eyed the cereal boxes. "Any other cereal?"

His father shook his head.

Owen pulled a face. "This is healthy stuff that makes you go to the toilet."

Chantel, who had stretched out her hand toward a box, pulled it back.

Everyone laughed.

"Hope you all like four-minute eggs," said Lynne, appearing with a tray of eggcups.

"Did you see the newspaper?" Ron asked Lynne as she joined them at the table.

"Only the headlines."

Ron pulled out one of the inside pages and handed it to Lynne. "There's a story on Savernake Forest about a plan to widen the road by cutting down some trees."

"What?" Holly jerked upright. "Not the big old oak hanging over the road?"

All the children froze in mid bite.

Lynne squinted at the photo and the story. "It could be," she said slowly. "It's hard to tell from a newspaper photo." She pushed the page across the table.

Holly pounced and scanned the picture and text. "I knew it! They're going to cut down the Mother Tree." A weird look crossed her face and she thrust her hand in her jeans pocket. "That must be why this tape was tied on one of the branches. It was a marker."

"You removed it?" Lynne tutted.

Holly nodded. "It looked out of place so I pulled it off.

But it's proof isn't it? It was a marker for a tree they're going to cut down." She thumped the table. "We've got to stop them."

"Don't get your knickers in a twist," said Owen. "It could be a marker for a tree they wanted to save."

Holly looked at him in consternation. "OH NO, then they won't know which one!"

"Either way, you can't do anything about it," interjected her father.

"Yes we can!" Holly waved the paper frantically. "There's a rally to save the forest. It's tomorrow. Will you take us? Please, Dad? It's not far, remember, just beyond Marlborough. Please?"

Ron stood up and shook out his napkin. "Sorry, Holly. I'm here to work." He tried to smooth things over. "But I bet the tree-cutting idea has upset a lot of people. There's mention of petitions being circulated. Why don't you see if there's one in the village? You could sign it."

Holly swung around to her mother. "Can *you* drive us? You love trees. Help save them."

Lynne shook her head. "Your dad needs the car, Holly."

Holly stared around the table. "I don't believe this. People want to cut down some of the oldest trees in Britain, and you're going to stand by and let them! Well I'm not standing by. I'm going to stop them." Holly flounced out.

Adam took advantage of the fuss to mutter thanks and also disappear from the table.

"Holly! Adam!" called Owen. "Wait . . . what about the museum?" They were gone before he could finish.

Ron grinned at his wife. "Have a nice day." He bent down and pecked her cheek.

Lynne pulled a face.

Holly sprinted across the garden and sped the width of the field to the stones.

Running didn't help; she was still seething. She jogged along the edge of the ditch and around the entire Stone Circle. It was early. No other visitors had arrived yet to see the stones. She had them to herself.

She stared at each stone as she jogged past. Each had its own character. On some, the surface planes and ridges made faces. One sported the profile of an Egyptian Sphinx, another, the head of a lion. But even though she was amazed by their presence and sensed their magic, she didn't feel them call her as Owen did. It was the voice of the Mother Tree that she heard in her head.

Holly suddenly detoured through the village and paused to read the notice board at the post office; then she took off again and finished the circuit. Breathless, she flung herself down behind the stone nearest to the house and stared unseeing up at the sky.

She *had* to go to the forest. The Mother Tree haunted her. Its branches reached out. She could feel it, smell it, hear its voice calling. She *would* help save it. Holly took the acorn out of her pocket and turned it over and over. "I must get there," she whispered.

"Get where, the forest?" Adam's shadow fell across Holly as he appeared from the other side of the stone.

Holly jumped. "I didn't know you were here."

"I didn't know you were till you spoke," Adam countered. He sat down on the grass beside her.

"I'm really mad," admitted Holly.

"Me too," sighed Adam.

There was a long silence as they both stared over the ditch and into the distance.

The sun warmed their skin, a lark sang and through their backs came the faint comforting throb of the stones.

Holly sighed and looked sideways at Adam. "Want to talk about it?"

Adam shrugged. "It won't help. You can't do anything about the Wise Ones ignoring me."

"Oh, Adam, don't be daft. They're not ignoring you any more than they're ignoring me. It's just that Chantel was the first to see Equus. As for Owen . . . Well, you were with us in the Place Beyond Morning. You must have seen how he looked at Ava."

"How?" said Adam.

"Don't be dense! Owen's gaga about Ava. He'll do anything for her. Don't you remember? He told her she was beautiful."

Adam nodded slowly. "She is beautiful, but she's kind of scary."

"Owen didn't think so . . . they just clicked. So of course she called on him for help. They made a connection, just like Equus and Chantel."

"So you don't think I'm being punished because I failed in the last adventure?"

Holly rolled on her side and stared at Adam. "You didn't fail; you were really strong. You overcame the dragon when it was twisting your mind. I don't think I could have done that."

Adam's body relaxed. "I thought I'd screwed up."

"Oh, don't be stupid." Holly grinned and gave him a friendly punch. "Work on your inferiority complex."

Adam grinned back. "Okay, okay, but it would be easier if I had something to do."

"You can think of a way to get me to Savernake Forest."

Adam wrinkled his forehead. "Bus?"

"I checked the timetable in the village. The country bus doesn't run very often, and it only goes to Marlborough, not to the forest."

"How far is it? Could you go on your bike?"

"Adam Maxwell, you are brilliant. It can't be more than fifteen miles away." Holly paused. "If you could get out the bike and helmet as though you're going to ride around the village, then pass it to me, Mum won't guess." Holly started to tick items off on her fingers. "I'll need a map . . . and some money . . . and a water bottle . . . and lunch."

Adam frowned. "Shouldn't you tell someone where you're going?"

"I've told you, haven't I?"

"Guess so."

"If I'm not back by teatime, you can send out a search party."

"I'll help on one condition."

Holly raised an eyebrow. "Condition?"

"I go with you!"

"You're mad. There'll be a row."

"They'll be even more furious if you go on your own."

Holly pursed her lips. "True." She turned a puzzled glance at Adam. "Why do you want to stick your neck out?"

Adam hunched his shoulders. "There's nothing better

to do, and I guess I don't feel part of this Circle stuff."

"I know what you mean. I've been obsessed by the Mother Tree, but I couldn't figure out where it fitted in with Ava and the Circle." Holly chewed her lip. "I keep remembering how the dragon sucked you in with Dark Magic." She looked guiltily at Adam. "I wondered if I was making the same mistake. I'm so glad the Forest Magic and Circle Magic are linked with mistletoe. Forest Magic feels right."

"Deep down, I always sensed the dragon was wrong," admitted Adam.

"Deep down, I know I've got to help the Mother Tree," said Holly.

"Then let's both go to the rally to support her and bring back some mistletoe for Ava," urged Adam. "Chantel and Owen will cover up for us."

"All right," said Holly.

Adam slapped her shoulder. "Race you to Manor Cottage." He took off before Holly could scramble to her feet.

The wraith flowed restlessly around its earthy cell, thrusting misty tendrils in cracks and fissures, searching for weakness. It felt stronger. Last night's dark had brought the strange power again. Not full power though. The wraith withdrew its tendrils as though they burned. The summer sun was so strong it warmed the earth and made the darkness shudder.

Dimly the wraith remembered a time when it had roamed freely in the light. Twice it had melded with other beings and disrupted the Circle's power. Once as a boar it had tried to destroy the rituals, and once as a human it had almost succeeded in damaging the stones. The wraith shuddered, remembering. The stones had struck back. One had fallen, crushing the human the wraith had inhabited.

The wraith loathed humans and hated the stones and the Wise Ones. It wanted the binding power of the circlet, but couldn't penetrate inside the Stone Circle. The last two nights, though, had brought a wicked hope. Its strength was growing again, and it knew how to use it. It would meld with a child. In the past, the stones had caused the death of an animal and a human adult, but they would never hurt a child.

Chantel looked small and lonely as she sat among the devastation of family breakfast. Her broken leg rested on the seat of the chair next to her and she gazed into space, chewing slowly.

Owen flicked a crumb at her and vanished into the kitchen with a pile of dirty dishes.

Chantel smiled slightly and took another nibble of her toast.

"What's up?" Owen reappeared to collect the last few plates.

Chantel pushed hers over to him. "Nothing."

"Must be something. You look like a wet Whit week."

Chantel looked blank. "What?"

"It's a saying. There's a Whit Week holiday in spring, and it always rains, so everyone is miserable."

"Oh," said Chantel.

"Well, that was a success!" said Owen. He picked up the remaining dishes and vanished again.

Chantel sighed, lowered her cast and clumped into the kitchen to join him.

Owen was up to his elbows in soapsuds, piling clean dishes haphazardly on the draining board.

Chantel picked up a tea cloth and began to dry.

"Thanks," said Owen. "I decided if I wash up today, I'll be off the hook tomorrow."

"Good plan," said Chantel.

They worked together in silence.

Owen flicked some suds at Chantel. "Come on," he said. "What's up? You might as well tell me. Your face is a dead giveaway."

Chantel gave an embarrassed laugh. "Nothing really . . . except . . . I was thinking."

"About what?"

"Yesterday . . . at the stone where I felt ill. It wasn't sunstroke. I know it wasn't!" Chantel's soft voice was unusually forceful.

"So what was it?"

"Something that hated me. Something that wanted to hurt me."

"Like what?" persisted Owen.

Chantel gave a little shrug. "Maybe . . . I wondered . . ." Her voice dropped lower and lower until Owen could barely hear. "What if it's that wraith thing that Ava told you about?"

Owen tipped the basin of dirty water down the sink and dried his hands. "Mum," he hollered, "we're going out to the Circle, okay?" Without waiting for the answer, Owen opened the back door. "Come on. We'll find out."

"How?" Chantel hung back.

"You've not got sunstroke now, have you?"

Chantel shook her head.

"So you could walk toward the stone and see if the feeling crept up on you again."

Chantel didn't move.

"You a scaredy cat?"

Chantel jutted her chin. "No. But it made me feel bad. Besides, Equus said we should stay away until we know for sure what it is."

"How else do we find out if it's sunstroke or not?" Owen was reasonable but unbending. "All you have to do is start approaching it."

Chantel sighed. She looked at Owen with haunted eyes. "If it makes me feel awful, promise you'll help me get away? Promise?"

"Promise. Want to take the Bath chair?"

7.
THE NAMING DAY

Owen pushed the Bath chair across the road and Chantel steered expertly through the field gate. Neither noticed the hawk perched in the shadow of the post office chimney pot.

Adam sprinted over. "Where are you going?" he asked breathlessly.

"To conduct an experiment." Owen grinned. "Want to come?"

"Adam Maxwell, that wasn't a fair race," grumbled Holly, running up behind them.

"Got to be quick off the mark," said Adam, laughing. He turned back to Owen. "What's the experiment?"

"It's me who's doing it, if you don't mind." Chantel's voice came from inside the Bath chair.

Holly and Adam peered around the hood. Chantel was sitting bolt upright against the crimson leather cushions, looking offended.

Holly chuckled. "You look like the queen."

Chantel grinned, lifted her hand and gave a couple of

royal waves. She turned serious again. "We're going to the stone where I had sunstroke. I think the wraith Owen saw in his dream might have made me ill. I'm going to walk toward it and see if it makes me start to feel bad again." She sighed. "Owen says this is the best way to find out."

"I don't get it," said Adam.

"If it was sunstroke, nothing will happen," said Owen. "She's not ill now."

"What if it's not the wraith but something else weird? How will you know?"

Owen shrugged. "At least we can prove something's there." He trundled the Bath chair toward the trouble spot with Holly and Adam helping. "Ava said the wraith couldn't enter the Circle, but prowled around the outside, so we'll stay on the outside of the stones like we did before."

They stopped one stone away.

Chantel climbed out of the Bath chair and wedged her crutches under her arms. "Promise to help me if I feel ill."

"We will," the others chorused.

One step at a time, Chantel moved forward.

Nothing happened.

She took several more steps but felt nothing even though the stone loomed ahead. She looked back at the others. "Maybe it *was* sunstroke."

"Told you," crowed Adam.

She took a couple more steps, still nothing.

Then she stepped into the stone's shadow.

It was as though she had fallen into a cold black vortex. She uttered a strangled cry, her knees buckled, her hands lost their grip on the crutches and she started to collapse.

"Grab her," yelled Holly.

"Watch her leg," warned Adam.

The three cousins pounced and caught Chantel before she hit the ground. They dragged her back to the adjacent stone and propped up her head and shoulders.

Holly knelt and patted her cheeks. "Chantel, what happened?"

"Say something. Open your eyes," encouraged Adam. "Come on, Chantel."

Chantel's head moved sluggishly from side to side and her eyelids flickered. Her mouth opened and shut as though she was trying to say something, but no sound came out.

The cold black void swirled around her. Not the clean crisp coldness of ice, but a cold emptiness. Tendrils of blackness grasped at her heart and mind, squeezing out good thoughts and filling her with hate.

She struggled to keep an image, a word, something that meant hope and rescue. The word "Equus" floated for a second, but she couldn't remember what it meant. She opened her mouth to shout the word, but no sooner had the thought flickered than the coldness clamped around her heart even harder. She drifted into nothingness.

Then out of the black emptiness came a dark sense of purpose. She must enter the Circle and destroy the hidden power.

"She's just fainted . . . hasn't she?" asked Owen.

"Something's wrong." Adam's voice wobbled. "We should

have believed her. Now we've done it." He leaned forward and held her hands. "Chantel, Chantel, can you hear me?"

Chantel raised her head and her eyes opened.

Adam dropped her hands in shock and Holly and Owen moved back with a gasp of horror.

Chantel's eyes were black instead of green, and they gleamed with malevolence. Like an automaton, she attempted to rise, but was stopped by her leg. The black eyes traveled downward and rested on the cast as though seeing it for the first time. Her mouth sneered. She rolled onto her hands and knees and, dragging the broken leg behind her, began to crawl between the stones to enter the Circle.

"The wraith's got her. Stop her entering the Circle!" yelled Owen. He gripped Chantel's ankle.

Holly reacted instinctively. She snatched the acorn from her pocket and flung it at Chantel. "Lhiat myr hoilloo!" she yelled. "To thee as thou deservest!"

The acorn hit Chantel's cheek and shattered into fragments that hung in the air. A faint green light flickered over her body. The black eyes closed and her head slumped. She exhaled and a puff of gray mist left her lips. She sprawled on the ground.

The acorn shards collected around the mist, gathering and enclosing it. Whole again, the acorn fell to the grass and rolled toward Holly's feet.

"Did . . . did . . . that really happen?" whispered Adam. His face was ashen.

Holly only nodded. She stared down at the acorn but made no attempt to pick it up.

Owen gazed at Chantel, his mouth open. "That thing . . . it . . . it . . . "

Chantel's eyes flickered. "The wraith . . . I . . . has it gone?" Her voice was a tiny whisper and she shivered. She lifted her head, and her eyes opened. They were clear green. "Please . . . can we sit inside the Circle, in the sunshine?"

No one stirred. They stared at her.

The freckles stood out against Chantel's white skin, and dark shadows smudged beneath her eyes, but everyone's gaze was held by the small red mark on her cheek left by the acorn.

"Where's the . . . the . . . th th . . . thing?" stammered Owen.

"In that." Holly pointed toward the acorn.

Still no one moved.

Finally Adam stepped forward and helped Chantel up. His arm supported her waist as they walked slowly around the stone and sat down again.

Holly and Owen joined them.

"I . . . I . . . I'm so sorry. This was my fault. I . . . I didn't mean . . . " Owen stammered.

Chantel shook her head and gave him a tiny smile. She leaned her back against the stone, closed her eyes and tilted her face toward the sunshine with a sign of relief.

The other three also closed their eyes and leaned back with a sigh. It *was* better. A feeling of peace, a current of quiet energy, ran around the inside of the Circle. The sunshine warmed them. Their breathing slowed. They listened to the steady heartbeat of the stone and let it heal them.

The high sweet sounds of a penny whistle and singing roused

them. One by one the cousins opened their eyes. The music seemed to be coming from the direction of the Avenue.

At first there was nothing to see. Then a man with long gray hair and a gray beard appeared between the two large entrance stones. He carried a carved wooden staff with an ornate brass top. He turned and looked down the Avenue, raising his arms and the staff in a gesture of welcome.

Women wearing flowing dresses and wreaths of flowers in their hair, and men with oak leaves garlanding their necks, streamed through the Avenue entrance and milled around in the center of the Circle.

Gradually a procession formed. Everyone began to dance, weaving in and out between the stones, led by the long-haired girl in a black crop top and swirling skirt, playing the penny whistle.

A man with a guitar joined the girl, a fiddler followed and several people gathered behind playing small hand drums

Holly sat up straight. She recognized the girl as the one they had bumped into with the Bath chair. She nudged Owen.

He grinned.

"Is this one of Ava's dreams?" whispered Adam.

"No." Owen leaned over and pinched Adam.

"Ow." Adam rubbed his arm. "Guess you're right." He looked again at the gathering crowd. "That guy with the beard and stick, he's the weirdo we saw when we arrived!"

"And . . . ?" prompted Owen.

Adam looked blank. Owen pointed to the long-haired penny whistle player. Adam groaned.

"They've got a baby with them," said Chantel. She'd spotted a woman dipping and swaying behind the penny whistle player. The woman held the child in her arms and presented it to each stone as she danced past.

Several visitors from the tour buses arrived. Instead of photographing the stones they rushed across the field, cameras pointed at the dancers.

"The dancers are coming this way." Holly jumped up. "What if they step on the acorn?" The children looked at each other in horror. They peered around their stone. The acorn still lay on the grass. No one moved to pick it up.

"We can't leave it there." Holly took a deep breath. "Owen lend me your hankie."

Owen pulled a crumpled and stained square out of his pocket and handed it over.

"Yuck!" said Holly. "You might have washed it when you washed the rest of your clothes."

"I did," said Owen. "It was in my pocket."

Holly ignored him. She dropped the hankie beside the acorn, picked up a twig and nudged the acorn onto the fabric.

Suddenly they were surrounded by dancers and singers.

"Blow away the morning dew. The dew, oh the dew . . ." they sang.

Holly panicked and kicked the acorn out of the way, into a hollow at the base of the stone.

"Blow away the morning dew. How sweet the winds do blow."

"Ah, more children of the stones. How sweet. Come and celebrate Rosie Dawn's naming day with us," said the woman with the baby.

A couple of young men swept Owen off, thrusting a drum into his hands.

Two teenage girls clasped Holly's hands and waltzed her around the stone. Crystals flashed from ears and chains around necks.

"No . . . no . . . " Holly protested, but a laughing woman placed a wreath on her head and the fiddler struck up a new verse.

> There is a flower in our garden
> That's called the Marigay,
> And if thou shalt not when thou can,
> Thou canst not when thou may.
> Oh, blow away the morning dew . . .

The air rang with song.

The girls tugged her along as they headed for the next stone.

Holly gave up and danced doggedly between them.

Only Adam stood his ground. Or tried to. "Stop it," he yelled in fury. "Can't you see my sister's broken her leg?"

A garlanded youth pushed the Bath chair to Chantel's side. Gentle hands lifted her in. She was showered with rose petals and pushed around the stones.

"Come on, Adam," she shouted, her head poking out around the hood. "Join in. It's a Circle Dance."

"No way," yelled Adam over the music. No one heard him. The crush of dancers absorbed the Bath chair. He lost sight of it.

Adam clenched his fists. "Everyone in England's mad," he muttered.

"Relax, son." A hand patted his shoulder. Adam swung around and came face to face with the bearded man holding the staff.

"Leave your anger outside the Circle, especially today."

"Who are you, and what's so great about today?" said Adam.

"It's a day of happiness, a child's naming day. I'm performing the ceremony." The man stuck out his hand. "Dave, Keeper of the Stones."

Adam looked blank.

"Dave the Druid."

Adam took off at a run, back to the refuge of Manor Cottage.

The dancers, musicians and celebrants tripped through the gate and across the village street to the next section of the Great Circle.

A peaceful silence fell.

A hawk circled above, swooped and landed on the ground near the stone that marked the wraith's cell. She scratched in the grass at the stone's base. Grasping the acorn in her beak, she took to the air. Circling low over the big barn in the museum complex, the hawk got her bearings and flapped off across the Circle toward Savernake Forest.

In the woods behind the barn lurked a youth with a slingshot. He had spent the afternoon picking off rooks, but a hawk was better prey.

He aimed and let fly, just as the bird's course took her above the dancers.

The stone hit her on the breastbone.

Ava gasped. The acorn fell from her beak and her wings lost their rhythm. She fought the pain, forcing her wings to tilt and turn her body. She half-glided, half-fell from the sky onto the roof of the barn.

As it neared the ground, the acorn glanced off the shoulder of the long-haired girl playing the penny whistle.

"Ouch," said the girl. She stomped on the nut and carried on, failing to notice the faint mist that rose from the shards and surrounded her body.

"Does this happen often, Auntie Lynne?"

Adam and his aunt stood at the garden gate of Manor Cottage, looking over the field.

The naming day celebration had moved to their side of the Circle. A large audience of visitors and villagers had gathered to watch. Like Holly, Owen and Chantel, many onlookers had joined in.

Lynne chuckled. "People often use the Circle for weddings and christenings . . . What did you say they were calling this?"

"A naming day for Rosie Dawn." Adam's voice was full of revulsion.

Lynne patted his shoulder. "Don't be prejudiced. It's not your thing, but how nice that people are still using the Circle for celebration. That's probably what it was built for."

She shaded her eyes to watch two men in the middle of the field. They carried a tall pole that they wedged upright in a wooden stand. One loosened a string, and a profusion of colorful ribbons showered down from the top.

"Lovely, a Maypole dance!" said Lynne. "I'm going for my camera." She ran inside and reappeared a few minutes later, the camera dangling from her hand.

"Coming, Adam?"

Adam shook his head but opened the gate for her. He

watched as Lynne ran across the field to record the festivities. She passed by the long-haired girl who had stopped playing her whistle and was rubbing her forehead as though she had a headache.

The fiddle struck up a new tune.

Haste to the Maypole, haste away,
For 'tis now our holiday.

Voices soared as dancers grabbed the ribbons and wove in and out, under and over, forming a colorful braid down the pole.

"Excuse me. Yoohoo." The voice came from nearby. "Aye, kid . . . It's you I'm talking to."

Adam leaned out over the gate.

A man and woman, obviously part of the naming day celebrations, pushed a wheelbarrow containing coils of bright green garden hose.

They stopped and the woman brushed back long tendrils of hair from her face. "This is Manor Cottage, isn't it?" she said breathlessly.

Adam nodded.

The man pointed to the hose. "The Prendergasts said we could hook up to their water tap."

Adam looked nonplussed. He shrugged.

"Hold the gate then, mate." The couple maneuvered the wheelbarrow through.

Adam watched as they attached the hose to a tap in the back wall and started wheeling the barrow back, uncoiling as they went.

Adam couldn't help but be curious. "What do you need water for?"

"So everyone can toast Rosie Dawn." The woman smiled. "There's a lot of people out there. You're welcome to join us."

Adam shook his head. "No thanks," he said, but couldn't resist another comment. "I thought toasts were done with wine."

The couple chuckled.

"Water's the wine of the gods . . . a gift from the earth," said the man.

"Especially Avebury water," added the woman. "This is the ancients' magical water. Water from the stream that doesn't run."

Bemused, Adam watched as they ran the hose to the center of the field, where a woman had spread a white linen cloth on the ground. In the middle stood a large silver goblet. Beside it she had placed an empty punch bowl and a basket full of paper cups.

"They're all mad . . . totally mad," said Adam to himself. He took refuge in the cottage, shutting the door firmly on the revelries.

***

It was no use. Adam couldn't settle. The strains of the embarrassing pageantry were loud and clear. He decided to go to the museum, but couldn't remember where Holly had left the tickets. After a short search he gave up and left a note on the kitchen table. *Gone biking. Will stay in reach of village.* He extracted one of the bikes from the stable and wheeled it outside.

The village street was deserted. All the visitors were watching the ceremony. The only person around was Mrs. Bates, the owner of the antique shop. She sat beside her door, enjoying the sunshine. "That Bath chair still going strong?" she called out.

"Yup." Adam wheeled the bike across the road and chatted with her while buckling on his helmet.

"Well, young fellow, not joining in the dancing?"

Adam pulled a face and shook his head.

Mrs. Bates chuckled. "Aw, they're all right, that lot. Don't do no harm. Clean up after themselves and bring a lot of custom our way."

Adam's eyes widened. "There's no one here."

Mrs. Bates rubbed her hands together. "Wait until that lot's finished. Everyone'll be in a feel-good mood and ready to spend a few pennies."

"Who are they? Do they often come here."

"New Agers, that's who." Mrs. Bates took a roll of mints from her pocket, popped one in her mouth and offered the roll to Adam.

They sucked companionably.

"They come on what they call the old feast days." Mrs. Bates ticked them off on her fingers. "Winter Solstice, Summer Solstice, Lammas, Beltane, Imbolc, Candlemas, full moon, can't remember them all. Then there's naming ceremonies and bonding ceremonies, seems like every month there's something big. What is it today?"

"A naming ceremony," said Adam.

Mrs. Bates chuckled. "What's the poor kid called this time?"

Adam grinned. "Rosie Dawn."

"Hmmm, not bad . . . she'll be plain old Rosie at school. Last one was called Micklemas. Bet the poor lad's Mickey Mouse for the rest of his days."

Adam guffawed, then decided to ask about something he didn't understand. "They're getting water from the Prendergasts' for a toast."

Mrs. Bates gave a nod. "That's what they usually do. Got to have the four elements, see."

"The four elements?" Adam was suddenly alert.

"Earth, air, fire and water. Can't do rituals without them. Been used for thousands of years."

Adam tucked the information away. Wait till the others heard! What else did Mrs. Bates know? he wondered. "What's so special about the water? They said it was magic water, from the stream that doesn't run."

"That's right enough. Go and take a look-see. Interesting river, the Kennet. It's running now, but come back in the winter months and there'll be nought there. Yon stream bed'll be dry as a bone."

Adam raised his eyebrows.

Mrs. Bates pointed. "Ride down to the bottom of the street, but when the road stops, go through the footpath between the hedges and ride along until you reach the wooden bridge. Take a look-see. That'll be the magic River Kennet."

"Okay . . . thanks," said Adam.

The stream wasn't far. Adam rode beyond the museum buildings, past the church and manor, then between two laurel hedges taller than himself. Suddenly he was on the bridge.

He stopped, propped the bike against the wooden parapet and leaned over.

The Kennet sparkled and danced under the bridge like any other stream. He tried to figure it out. In a dry summer the stream was running, so why wouldn't it run in the winter when there was rain?

He scratched his head. This needed thought.

A grin spread across Adam's face. He'd solved something from Owen's dream. He was one up on the others! He'd found out about the four elements. It wasn't mistletoe; it was earth, air, fire and water. Not only that, he knew what was meant by "water from the stream that didn't run."

8.
THE NIGHT OF DESTRUCTION

"Where's Adam?" asked Owen.

Adam entered the kitchen just as Holly picked up the note from the kitchen table and waved it under Owen's nose.

"I'm back," Adam announced.

"You missed out," said Chantel.

Adam snorted.

"No really," Chantel insisted. "The naming ceremony was great." Her cheeks were flushed and her eyes sparkled. A few stray rose petals still dotted her hair. "I wish I'd had a naming day like that." She sighed longingly. "Rosie Dawn's a beautiful name."

"You're no judge," said Adam. "You called a doll Marshmallow."

"So? I was three. And she was soft and squishy," said Chantel defensively as everyone laughed.

Holly's wreath had slipped over one eye. She pulled it off and wound it artistically around a candlestick. "It was fun. They blessed the baby and showered her with rose petals. The man with the staff, Dave . . . "

"Dave the Druid," interrupted Adam, laughing rudely.

"Dave the Druid," said Holly equably, "called in the four directions as witnesses and we all toasted the baby with drinks of water."

"It was beautiful," said Chantel dreamily, "and there's going to be dancing and music all day."

Adam rolled his eyes.

Lynne placed her camera on the counter. "Life certainly isn't dull in this village. What's next on the agenda?"

"Food!" came the cry.

They all busied themselves making sandwiches.

Holly pulled the passes out of her pocket. "Are we going to the museum this afternoon?" she mumbled with her mouth full.

Her mother coughed warningly.

Holly swallowed. "Well? Are we?"

"Sure," said Adam.

The others looked at him in surprise.

"You're in a good mood," observed Owen. He rinsed his plate and leaned it up to dry.

Adam followed suit. "Got something to tell you . . . about your dream," he said.

Both boys slipped out to the patio.

"What's the big secret?" Holly and Chantel had followed close behind.

"Keep your voices down! I've found out the answer to Owen's dream. When the shaman talked about water from the stream that didn't run."

Everyone looked expectantly at Adam.

"Well, there really is one!"

"What, a stream that doesn't run?" echoed Owen.

"Yup. It's just outside the village. The River Kennet runs in the summer but dries up in the winter."

"No. You've got it the wrong way round," said Holly. "Streams dry up in the summer and run in the winter."

"Not the Kennet," said Adam triumphantly. "I guess that's why it's supposed to be magic. Go see. It's running now, but Mrs. Bates says it doesn't run in the winter."

"Weird." Holly furrowed her brow. "There must be an explanation."

Adam shrugged. "Sure, there must. But in ancient times it would seem like magic, right?"

"Right," agreed Owen.

"That's not all. There should be four elements in a ritual and I know what they are, earth, air, fire and water. Mrs. Bates told me." Adam glanced uneasily at Holly. "She didn't say anything about mistletoe, though."

"Earth, fire and water were in Owen's dream. So was mistletoe," said Holly slowly. "But was mistletoe air?"

There was silence while everyone thought.

Owen suddenly pulled the feather from his pocket and waved it. "This was air . . . the hawk-headed shaman used a feather. Birds fly in the air and Ava flies! Hey . . . what if Ava's air?"

"Earth, air, fire and water," said Holly slowly. "It sounds right. Ava could symbolize air . . . but what was the White Horse?"

"Earth," said Chantel.

Everyone stared at her.

"The White Horse and the Red Mare were carved in earth," Chantel explained patiently. "Everything was earth. The talisman was buried, the dragon was buried and Adam had to go underground to see Wayland. So Equus is earth."

"That can't be right. If Equus is earth and Ava is air, what about fire and water? There are only three Wise Ones," said Adam.

Holly shook her head. "There are four," she said firmly.

"No." Adam ticked them off on his fingers. "Equus, the horse; Ava, the hawk woman; and the old man, Myrddin. Three Wise Ones."

Holly shook her head. "There are four. I know it. I don't know how or why. I just know it." She pressed the sides of her head with both hands. "It's like something inside is telling me." She dropped her hands and continued with utter conviction, "There are four Wise Ones, and Myrddin is fire and the other is water."

Owen and Adam looked unconvinced, but Chantel touched Holly's arm and they exchanged quick smiles.

Owen shrugged. "Then the mistletoe must mean something else." He punched Adam's arm. "Thanks, Adam!"

***

The long-haired girl staggered as another wave of dizziness hit her. She thrust the penny whistle at the musician beside her. " I must have sunstroke," she muttered and stumbled to the shade of a tree at the edge of the field.

She sat on the grass and leaned against the trunk. The

dizziness grew worse. She closed her eyes and a shiver ran through her body. Blackness gathered and she was sucked down into an icy swirling void.

She surfaced angrily. Angry that she had got sunstroke, angry at the stones because it was their fault, and angry at . . . at . . . her mind cast around trying to make sense of her anger . . . Aaah! She was angry at those kids who'd run into her. They laughed when she dropped her ice cream. How dared they?

A rush of fury flooded her body. She'd get even with them if it were the last thing she did!

The girl clambered to her feet and swayed groggily. She'd find those bratty kids and teach them a lesson. Maybe they were among the people watching the festivities. She made her way unsteadily back to the edge of the Stone Circle and stared at every kid, but none of them were the right ones. She'd try looking in the village next.

※※※※

Following the arrows labeled MUSEUM, Owen, Holly and Adam pushed the Bath chair containing Chantel into a large cobbled courtyard surrounded by trees. Loud caws burst from the trees as they walked past.

"Crows?" asked Chantel.

"Rooks," said Owen. "Look." He ran under the trees and clapped his hands loudly.

With cries of alarm the rooks rose from the branches in a great black cloud and wheeled angrily overhead.

As soon as Owen had disturbed them he felt guilty. He shouldn't have frightened them. He'd been a bird last night.

He remembered the feel of the wind under his wings and his delight in the freedom of flight. Then he remembered how his heart had pounded in his chest when he was buffeted and blown in the snowstorm. He sent a mind message. "Sorry, rooks, I won't frighten you again." To his surprise, they immediately stopped their cries and settled back in the tree branches.

Adam pointed across the courtyard. Several wooden tables were filled with people eating and drinking. Behind them were the open doors of a converted stable. "Great, a restaurant. Let's see what's on the menu."

"We've just had lunch," protested Holly.

Owen backed up Adam. "There's always room for snacks."

"Later," insisted Holly, rolling her eyes toward Chantel. She marched into the doorway of the largest building. "Come on, show your passes."

The ticket collector waved through their passes but pointed to the Bath chair. "That stays outside. It's too big, but we've a wheelchair you can borrow."

"Thanks," said Chantel. She climbed out of the Bath chair and hopped over to the waiting wheelchair. "Hey, I like this." Spinning the wheels by hand, she propelled herself into the barn.

The others followed.

The barn was cool and dim after the brilliant sunshine. The thick stone walls and massive interior roof beams arched high over the children's heads.

"It's like being in a church," said Chantel softly as she gazed up into the shadows.

"Something up there moved," said Holly. Her voice echoed in the large space.

"Looking for our bats?" asked an interpreter.

"Bats?" said the children. They all stared intently at the roof.

"Occasionally one moves," continued the interpreter. "Or you hear the odd squeak, but they sleep during the day. The best time to see them is dusk, when they stream out of the vent holes to catch flying insects. It's quite a sight. There's been a bat colony in the barn for hundreds of years." She laughed. "We could only get permission to make the barn into a museum if we promised not to disturb the bats."

"Neat," said Holly.

"I'm Sue," said the interpreter. "You can come and ask me anything you like about Avebury."

"I want to know about the Stone Circle," said Owen eagerly. "Who built it, and why are so many stones missing?"

The interpreter pointed to a small ramp. "If you go up the ramp you'll find information about the builders. Then move to the middle of the barn for information about the Barber Surgeon and how he helped destroy the stones."

"Barber Surgeon?" questioned Chantel.

Sue smiled. "Yes, a man who wandered from village to village pulling teeth, lancing boils and cutting hair. He made quite an impact on Avebury."

"Thanks." Owen flashed her a smile and ran up the ramp.

He stopped short and pointed. "I don't believe it! That could be Hewll!"

A life-sized model of a man with long hair, wearing a leather tunic and a woolen wrap, stared at them. He was holding an antler pick in his hand as if about to strike. Below the model were a couple more antler picks and some scapula shovels. Above them a sign said "Please Touch." "Those clothes, the antler pick, it's just like my dream," whispered Owen.

Adam picked up an antler pick and swung it experimentally. Holly tried hefting a bone shovel.

Chantel picked up a stone hammer and banged repeatedly on a log provided for the purpose. The stone head wobbled and fell off as the leather binding loosened. Chantel looked embarrassed and dropped the handle back on the display table. "It's hard to believe the ditch and Stone Circle were made with these tools. The Circle is so massive and the tools so . . . so . . . " she searched for the right word, "so fragile."

Holly was reading the exhibit labels. "It took two thousand years to build the ditch and the Circle." Her voice was filled with awe. She lifted an antler pick again in her hand. "Making it must have been really important to the people who lived then."

"Of course it was," hissed Owen. "They'd promised Ava." He paused, a look of revelation on his face. "That's where the name comes from, isn't it? Ava's circlet is buried here . . . Avebury. Brilliant!"

He went charging off to see what else he could find.

Ava lay weakly on a rafter. She struggled to raise her head. Owen was near; she could sense him. He would help her, but they were running out of time. He needed one more clue for the ritual. If only she had enough strength to show him another glimpse of the past.

"Hey, Owen, here's the Barber Surgeon." Adam waved Owen over and pointed to a photo of human bones poking out from beneath a massive stone, and the rusted remains of ancient tools and a knife blade in a glass case. "This guy tried to wreck the stones, but they wrecked him. One fell on him and crushed him."

"Good for the stone," said Owen. He peered at the exhibit as Adam wandered off to the next section.

A strange feeling swept over him, a momentary dizziness as though his eyes weren't focusing properly, then a feeling of seeing things from far away. One moment Owen was leaning against the museum case, peering through the glass to look at the bones and read the story. The next minute the glass dissolved, the exhibit disappeared and it was as though he was hovering, hawk-like, above the Stone Circle, watching the past again!

It was a cold crisp midnight and the air smelled of Christmas. Mulled spices and cooking odors wafted from the open door of the Catherine Wheel Inn. Owen watched as the Barber Surgeon strode angrily out, his bag of knives and tools clinking on his belt. Behind him, drunken voices sang a raucous version of an ancient carol as the roasted head of a pig with an apple stuck in its mouth was hoisted onto the inn table.

The Boar's Head in hand bear I,
Bedecked with bays and rosemary,
And I pray you my masters be merry,
Quo estis in convivio.

The inn door slammed on the voices as the Barber Surgeon strode down the street toward the church, muttering, "'Tis blasphemous."

A bunch of children, boys in breeches and jerkins, girls in woolen kirtles and shawls, ran past him to gather around the church door as a lantern-lit procession emerged.

A fiddler led the way as the congregation, joined by the children, marched from the church, winding in and out of the great stones. The lanterns were placed against the stones, and the people moved to the center of the Circle. They held hands, made their own circle and began to dance, moving sedately first to the left, then to the right.

The Barber Surgeon followed and stood by a stone, glaring at them.

Owen noticed the faint mist gathering as the night-prowling wraith lurked on the edge of the Circle. He sucked in his breath, knowing what was likely to happen.

As the Barber Surgeon stood against a stone, the mist rose up around the man's feet and melded with him.

The Barber Surgeon watched and listened in anger and disbelief as the villagers raised their voices in song and tripped around and around.

Oh, the Holly bears a berry as white as the milk.
And Mary bore Jesus who was wrapped up in Silk.
Oh, Mary bore Jesus our Savior for to be.
And the first tree in the Greenwood, it was the Holly.
Holly, Holly.
Oh the first tree in the Greenwood, it was the Holly.

"DESIST!" The Barber Surgeon erupted into the middle of the dancers. Instead of just being angry, he'd suddenly become filled with a strange power. Power to change the world. "I will not stand by and watch blasphemy," he roared. "Where is your priest?"

The villagers stopped in bewilderment.

"He's in yon church, but he be coming along directly," said a cherry-cheeked woman. "We be celebrating Christmastide with the stones. Come, stranger, celebrate with us." She moved over to make a space.

"I will not!" shouted the Barber Surgeon. "The stones are evil. Who raised them?"

The people looked at each other and shrugged.

"Please, sir, they've always been here," said a youth.

"Could you have raised them?" the Barber Surgeon asked. The youth shook his head.

The Barber Surgeon pointed a finger at the biggest man, the smith. "You?"

The smith shook his great head. "Not I. 'Twould take stronger men than me."

"Only one person could raise this Circle. THE DEVIL!" roared the Barber Surgeon. "There is no place for the Devil's work in a Christian world." He pulled a crucifix from his jacket and held it up. "This place is cursed. I travel the length and breadth of England and never have I seen or felt a place so steeped in evil."

The villagers looked at each other in fear. They stepped back.

"Save yourselves before it is too late," roared the Barber Surgeon.

"How?" asked the smith.

"Topple and bury the stones. Let the blessed church protect you instead. The stones must be destroyed."

Owen watched the vision with disbelief as, exhorted by the stranger, who was now joined by the priest, the shocked villagers were bullied and browbeaten into fetching spades and picks and working through the night, digging deep holes into which they would topple the great stones.

"Don't do it," Owen whispered, but the people of the past couldn't hear.

The scene became a celebration as religious fervor enveloped the village. Fires were lit to soften the ground and provide light. The night took on a hideous glow. Then someone thought of laying fires at the base of the stones.

"Burn them like witches!" cried one woman.

"Yes, let them taste Hell," answered another.

"Watch me," boasted the smith. "Witness the art of the blacksmith. I know the magic of fire and water." He gestured to the observers. "Fetch water from the stream that does not run. Go to the village well."

A woman rushed to the inn courtyard and lowered a bucket into the deep stone-lined hole.

The drunken revelers spilled out from the inn to join their sober neighbors.

"Aye . . . what sport. Let's topple the stones," shouted a brawny farm worker. He brought forth a great hammer and swung it against the nearest stone. A chip flew and he laughed and swung again.

A stone, faggots blazing around its base, glowed with the heat.

"Bear witness to the power of the blacksmith," shouted the smith. He took the brimming bucket and dashed the icy cold contents against the hot rock. With a great crack the stone split in three pieces and fell to the ground.

A cheer went up.

The priest knelt and prayed with the stranger, giving thanks that this Christmas night had seen the old religion finally overthrown.

"Come . . . we need more men." The cry came from a group of shadowy figures struggling to push a large stone into a yawning pit at one side.

The priest and Barber Surgeon rose to their feet and ran to help.

All threw their full weight against the stone, but still it stood.

"Wait." The Barber Surgeon threw himself on the ground

and felt along the base of the stone. "There is a smaller stone preventing it. Hand me a pick." He leapt eagerly into the pit beneath the looming Sarsen.

The villagers watched aghast as the stone shifted and tipped of its own accord.

The ground shook as the great weight thudded down, crushing the Barber Surgeon before he could utter a word of protest.

Silence fell.

"The stones are angry," whispered a woman.

A man nodded. "This was a poor night's work. We will regret it."

One by one the villagers retreated, leaving the priest praying amidst fire and devastation. No one noticed a thin mist rise above the pit before being sucked swiftly back into the ground.

※✕✕◈✕✕※

The vision wavered and became smaller, dimmer. A moment's dizziness, and once again Owen was leaning against the glass case, staring at the bones and rusty knife. His eyes were moist. "How could they?" he muttered to himself. He blew his nose noisily. "And how come I'm seeing things without Ava's help?" He shook his head to clear it and moved away to find the others.

Owen . . . Owen! The voice in his head was a tiny sibilant squeak.

Owen stopped in mid-step. He looked around.

Holly and Chantel were still exploring the exhibit around Hewll. Sue the interpreter was talking to a person in the doorway. Adam was playing on a computer exhibit at the other side of the barn. No one else was within earshot.

A tingle ran up his spine. "Who's there?" he whispered.

The answer came back in short squeaky bursts of thought. *Me. Swoop. Friend of Ava. Mindspeak. I hear.*

Owen concentrated and spoke using his mind. *Where are you?*

Up . . . up.

Owen looked up. Hanging from the rafter was a small brown bat with bright eyes. It dropped from the beam and fluttered silently through the museum to the far corner of the barn.

Owen hurried after it.

Swoop hung from the corner of an exhibit case containing a computer simulation of the various stages of building Avebury.

Sit. I talk.

Owen settled on the bench opposite the screen.

Ava took acorn.

Owen gave a huge sigh of relief. *Ava saw what happened at the stone? Thank goodness. We were afraid to touch the acorn once the wraith was inside it.*

Ava hurt. Drop acorn.

WHAT . . . where is she?

Here. Sheltering. In roof, squeaked Swoop.

Owen stared up at the rafters. He could see nothing in the shadows. *Ava, are you up there? Did you send me the vision of the Barber Surgeon? Are you okay?*

Owen had a blinding flash of Ava's pain. He swayed on the bench. *AVA, what happened?*

113

Her mind touched his for only a moment as she tried to mindspeak. *King heal,* was all he got. It made no sense. He looked worriedly at the bat.

Help Ava. Swoop continued. *When museum shut. Come. Bring bag. Carry her.*

I'll come, promised Owen.

Take her. Gold King, squeaked Swoop.

Take her where? asked Owen.

Silbury Hill. Go sunset. Gold King help.

The Golden King, said Owen doubtfully. *King Sel? How are we supposed to find him?*

The bat ignored his question. *Go Silbury Hill. Sunset.* Swoop vanished into the shadows.

Owen tugged Adam's arm. "We've gotta go. Where are the girls?"

A puzzled Adam pointed around a screen at another set of exhibits. "There's still loads to see," he protested.

"Come on. It's important," insisted Owen. He ran over and whispered in the girls' ears.

"This better be good, Owen," grumbled Adam as the four of them huddled around one of the wooden tables outside.

"Good . . . it's terrible! But keep your voices down," Owen whispered. "Ava's hurt. Really hurt. I felt it." His voice was raw with worry. "She's sheltering in the roof of the barn with the bats. One of them's been talking to me. I've got to find Ava after the museum closes. I need a bag to carry her in."

The cousins gawked.

"I hope she's a hawk, not a woman," said Adam. "Or you'll need a pretty big bag."

"She's a hawk, stupid," said Owen. He paused. "I hope," he finished uncertainly.

Adam grinned.

"Adam, give over!" said Owen. "Or I won't tell you what else."

Adam sobered. "There's more?"

"Loads. She sent me a vision, about the Barber Surgeon! But the most important thing is to rescue her. The bat said to take Ava to Silbury Hill and the Golden King, at sunset."

Adam looked nonplussed. "Who?"

Holly nudged him. "Remember, Mum told us about Golden King Sel, the one who's buried under Silbury Hill."

Owen nodded eagerly. "That's the one. The bat says he'll help."

Adam shifted uneasily. "This is nuts. And I thought the last adventure was complicated!" He started ticking things off on his fingers. "Wise beings, dreams, a magic acorn, the Mother Tree, a wraith and stones that are supposed to dance. That was all complicated enough. Now suddenly Ava's hurt and there's a talking bat and a Golden King." He spread his hands in a gesture of despair. "It's too much. We've not even figured out the ritual yet. I can't keep track because everything's happening at once."

"'The light grows, but dark things stir,'" quoted Chantel softly. "It's the Old Magic waking everything up. Good things and bad things all happening at the same time."

"Let's hope nothing else wakes up, or we'll be toast," muttered Adam.

"How are we going to reach Ava?" asked Holly, sensible as always.

Owen shrugged. "Dunno yet."

Holly checked her watch. "The museum closes in about half an hour, but the sun won't set for ages. Why don't I take a bike and ride over to Silbury to check it out. It's only a mile away. I'll come back and report just after five. You go home and find a bag or something for Ava."

"A backpack would work, wouldn't it?" suggested Adam. "Will we need the first aid kit?"

"Good idea." Owen looked at Chantel. "Someone should stay and keep an eye on the barn. Do you want to do that?"

Chantel nodded. "We can hide Ava in the Bath chair to get her home," she suggested.

"Okay," Owen said. "I'll fill you all in later."

"Right. We'll meet back here in half an hour," said Holly.

She, Adam and Owen scattered.

The teenage girl paused in the village street. There was no sign of the children she was searching for. She rubbed her head again. She could remember nothing, not even why she was angry, but the anger drove her on. She walked up the lane toward the museum.

Suddenly, there was one of them, the small red-haired girl with the broken leg, sitting on her own in the courtyard. The girl who'd laughed! A wave of hatred swept over the teenager and wiped out all rational thought. The wraith's knowledge filled her mind. This was a Magic Child, a child linked to the stones' magic. A child who had resisted a melding. She was a threat and must be destroyed.

Chantel stared at the roof of the barn. What could have happened to Ava? How could a Wise One get hurt? They were invincible, weren't they?

She sat up straight. Something else was wrong. She could feel it. Something or someone was staring at her, hating her. It was the same feeling she had experienced from the wraith.

"Not again," she whispered and frantically looked around.

She saw nothing to alarm her. The museum barn, the stable block, all looked normal; none of the visitors was paying attention to her. Still the feeling persisted, eyes of hate boring into the back of her head.

Chantel extracted herself from the table and grabbed her crutches. She caught the glance of the long-haired teenage girl standing in the middle of the lane.

Eyes blazing, the girl stepped toward her.

Chantel shuddered and limped away from the table. She propelled herself across the yard in the opposite direction. She had no idea where she was going, just as far as possible from the mad-looking girl.

In a blind panic she moved rapidly beyond the barn and along a cobbled path. Suddenly there was a wall. She was trapped. No, she spotted a gate and a turnstile, the entrance to the manor grounds. Chantel waved her pass at the ticket collector and hobbled through with a sigh of relief.

The girl chasing her would have to stop to pay. That should give her time to hide.

"OY! Where do you think you're going?"

The teenage girl rattling the turnstile turned to stare at the ticket collector.

"Costs money to get in here." The man held out his hand. "Two pounds or get lost."

The girl fumbled in her pocket and pulled out a pile of change. She flung the coins toward the ticket collector and pushed again at the turnstile.

The ticket collector swore under his breath and clumsily bent down to pick up several coins that had fallen to the ground.

The girl rattled the turnstile again.

"Wait your patience," said the ticket collector, creakily standing upright. He released the catch.

The girl pushed through and took off at a run.

"OY, you," called the ticket collector. "You gave me too much."

The girl ignored him.

The manor grounds were large. Winding paths linked together yew walks and several small gardens. In between were expansive lawns with curving borders of flowers and stands of trees offering places to dodge behind.

Chantel could dodge no more. Her leg throbbed, her heart thumped and her breathing hurt. Whichever way she turned, the footsteps followed.

Panic-stricken, Chantel gazed around the garden she had just entered and realized she was cornered. This garden was walled on all sides; a single gate acted as both entrance and exit.

Frantically she looked for a place to hide. She was in a

topiary garden. Yew trees had been trimmed into fanciful shapes. Chantel's eyes passed rapidly over a lion, a peacock, a unicorn, a wild boar and a sphinx. The hedge beside her was carved into waves. Some small trees were shaped into diamonds and hearts. A knee-high spiral maze surrounded an ornamental pond in the middle of the garden.

Chantel's heart sank. Nothing here offered concealment. She turned to leave. Too late! She cowered behind the hedge as footsteps stopped at the garden entrance.

The girl peered through the arched entrance. Hanging ivy obscured her view. Swearing, she pulled it away from the wall and left it in a heap on the ground.

The waves of hatred filled the air.

"Equus, help," whispered Chantel, but no comforting presence enveloped her. A sob escaped her. "Ava! Trees! Someone help me. Where can I hide?"

With a rustle, the yew hedge beside her parted its branches and revealed a hollow cavity at its heart. Chantel edged inside. The branches gathered around, their dense green leaves hiding her from view.

"Thank you," Chantel whispered. She patted the dark central trunk.

The leaves rustled. "Welcome, Magic Child. Forest Magic is always yours to use."

"Forest Magic?" whispered Chantel. Her hand flew up to her cheek and touched the faint mark left by the acorn. "Of course!" Flooded with newfound courage, she stared intently between the leaves. As the teenage girl crept past, Chantel pointed a finger and whispered, "I hiat myr hoilloo. To thee as thou deservest!"

The girl stopped dead in her tracks. She turned her head to locate the source of the whisper, but was distracted by something catching at her ankle.

A thin tendril of ivy caught her sandal. She lifted her leg to pull it free, but a second tendril thrust up from the gravel and whipped around the other ankle. Within seconds, ivy was winding around her body, binding her legs and skirt, her chest, her arms, her hair and covering her face. It happened so fast that she made no sound. The topiary garden was now graced by a new sculpture in the center of the main path.

Owen and Adam ran back into the museum complex. Owen's pack bounced up and down on his back. Adam carried a first aid kit. They stopped at the empty table. Chantel was nowhere to be seen.

They hung around, scanning the people moving in and out of the restaurant.

"Where's she gone this time?" said Adam.

Chantel didn't reappear, but the abandoned Bath chair was still parked on its own by the barn wall.

Owen approached the next table. "Excuse me. Did you see a red-haired kid with a broken leg sitting at this table?"

The older woman nodded. "Yes, I noticed her. Was she waiting for you?"

Owen nodded. "Did you see where she went?"

The woman waved her hand vaguely beyond the museum. "That way, I think. I wasn't really watching."

"Thank you." Owen walked to the museum and poked his head inside. "Chantel," he called, "are you in here?"

Sue looked up, waved and shook her head.

Baffled, the two boys walked past the museum and toward the entrance to the manor gardens. Owen peered over the turnstile but didn't expect to see his cousin. She'd had no reason to go into the grounds.

"Looking for someone?" grunted the ticket collector.

"My cousin. She's got red hair and a cast on her leg."

"Oh aye, she came through about fifteen minutes ago. Just before the crazy girl."

"What girl?" said Adam.

"A teenager. Real rude she was. Flung the money at me and took off as though she was chasing something." The man stopped and scratched his chin. "That's funny. Come to think of it, your cousin seemed in a right old hurry too."

Owen fished in his pocket and pulled out his pass. "I'll fetch her. Thanks." He turned to Adam. "There's something going on," he hissed. "You get the Bath chair."

Adam nodded and ran back to the barn.

"We're closing in fifteen minutes, so don't you be long now. By rights I shouldn't be letting anyone else in," grumbled the ticket collector.

Owen smiled winningly. "My cousin's not got a watch, so I'll just find her and remind her what the time is."

The ticket collector grunted and released the turnstile.

Owen jogged rapidly through the gardens but saw no one. "Chantel," he hollered. "Where are you? It's nearly closing time."

Chantel stumbled out of the walled garden, tears of relief pouring down her face.

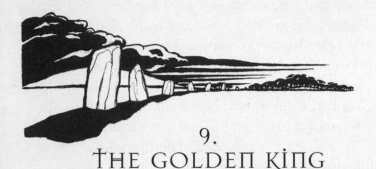

9.
THE GOLDEN KING

Myrddin raised his arms and pleaded with the heavens. "Equus, hear me! Return from the edge of the shadow!"

No answering hoofbeats echoed on the breath of the wind.

"Equus," roared Myrddin. "Listen to the wind. I dare not send mindspeak toward the shadow lest it be intercepted by the Dark Being." He strode around, stirring swirls of stardust with each swing of his cloak.

Only the endless songs of space and time hummed in his ears.

Myrddin muttered and tugged at his beard. "What to do? What to do next?" He peered down toward Gaia and sighed. "This is a sorry affair. Ava hurt and defenseless with only the children as support. Equus out of reach. As for me . . ." Myrddin shook his fist. "Myrddin the Great is helpless. All because a human child cannot open his eyes to see stardust or his ears to hear my voice."

He snatched a handful of the stardust from the swirl

around his body. "*But try I must, for I have nothing else to help us.*" *He flung it toward Gaia.* "*Child, expand your mind. See the light and believe. Time is running out. Light and Dark, Dark and Light. Help us now, for the light dims.*"

The dust sifted gently toward the earth.

"*Oh, for my staff,*" *Myrddin groaned, sinking his head in his hands.*

The stars shivered.

Holly pedaled furiously toward Silbury Hill. She could see it ahead, a great grass-covered mound towering over the trees.

She turned into the visitors' car park and dismounted, leaning the bike against the fence.

She wasn't the only visitor. Four cars were neatly parked and several people scattered around, either reading the Historic Site information boards or staring blankly up at the perfect green cone.

"That's it . . . Just a hill?" said one of the women.

Holly stared up at Silbury. The gigantic mound rose mysteriously from the valley floor. It was ancient and impressive but its symmetry had no obvious purpose. Her eyes raked its surface. She willed it to give a hint of its secret.

"We can't even climb up. There's a fence and notices everywhere. 'Keep off. This hill is unstable,'" muttered the woman's husband. "What's the point of coming?"

Holly sighed. The couple's comments reflected her own thoughts and didn't help solve her problem. She eyed the fence, wondering how Owen and Ava could slip through and up the hill for sunset. "Someone will see and stop them," she thought. "It's not like it's the dead of night."

She wandered around the fence at the base of the mound.

One by one the other visitors returned to their cars and drove off.

Holly reached the far side of the hill. The bulk was between her and the road, and she was far enough around the curve that the car park was out of sight. "Hmmm," she whispered to herself. "They might be able to get up this side. Hardly anyone would notice kids climbing here."

She tugged on the fence. The wires lifted. There was enough give for a child to wriggle underneath. She turned her back to the hill and surveyed the ground behind her.

A faint trace of a footpath snaked through the bushes beyond Silbury and wiggled through a line of trees between the fields. Holly grunted with satisfaction and kicked the nettles straggling over the path. It obviously wasn't very well used, and it headed toward Avebury.

Holly ran back to the car park to collect her bike. Pushing it through the rough grass at the base of the hill, she mounted at the footpath and patted the handlebars encouragingly. "Time to try dirt biking. If this path comes out where I think it does, we'll be able to sneak Ava out here at sunset." She set off to explore.

The restaurant was closed, the visitors gone and the wooden tables wiped and ready for the next day. With a protesting squeal the great doors of the barn swung shut and the lock clicked. Sue dropped the key into her duffel bag and swung it over her shoulder. She waved cheerily to Owen, Adam and Chantel sitting around a table. "Don't you kids have a home to go to?"

Owen smiled politely. "We're staying at Manor Cottage. Mum will holler when it's teatime." He pointed to the ducks dabbling in the small pond. "We're bird-watching."

"Good night then." Sue walked down the lane.

"Good night," the children replied. They watched until she disappeared around the corner.

"Bird-watching," sputtered Chantel. "That's a good one. Since when have you bird-watched?"

Owen gave a forced grin. "Since now. Sounded good, didn't it?" He checked around. Other than the children and the birds, the museum complex was finally deserted.

"I thought she'd never go," said Adam.

"Me too," Chantel said. She was still pale, but the color was returning to her cheeks. "What's next?"

Owen anxiously checked his watch. "Wait for Holly and Swoop."

With a tinkle of her bell, Holly rode into the courtyard. "Do you want the good news or the bad?"

Owen groaned. "More bad news?"

"Not really." Holly dropped the bike on the grass and joined them on the bench. "It's just that it's going to be tricky getting up Silbury Hill without being seen. It's all fenced, and no one's supposed to climb it."

"Oh, great. Now what?" Owen's shoulders slumped.

"The good news is I think I've figured out a way we could do it," Holly continued. "I've found a disused foot path, so we don't have to go by the road. We should have no trouble sneaking Ava there unseen." She looked over at the barn. "What's happening with Ava?"

Owen sighed. "I wish Swoop would hurry up and tell me. I'm really worried about her."

The children stared at the barn. No bats emerged.

"Myrddin." Ava's mindspeak was a weak flicker. "I cannot fly."

Myrddin groaned as he caught and held the mind picture she sent.

Ava lay slumped along a rafter in the great barn. The gash in her chest still oozed drops of bright red blood that pooled beneath her and matted her feathers. Her eyes were glazed, her feathers dull. Her beak hung open and she panted with rapid shallow breaths as though each breath hurt.

"Ava." Myrddin's voice was gentle. "Keep the light in your heart. The children will help."

"The darkness gathers behind my eyes. The light is dim," Ava whispered.

A band of grief tightened around Myrddin's chest. "Ava, concentrate on the light! You must not let it out. Our job is not yet done."

"Only . . . Golden King . . . can help me now." Ava's whispers came and went with the wind. "Send blessings, Myrddin, . . . tell . . . children . . . make . . . circle . . . "

She faded out.

Owen dragged his eyes away from the barn and looked at his sister and cousins. "You'd better hear what happened to Chantel."

Chantel's story shook them.

"We shouldn't have left you alone," Holly said.

"It's okay. You didn't know. No one did," said Chantel. "I just wish I knew why it happened."

"It must be something to do with the acorn," said Owen. "Swoop said Ava dropped it."

"If it dropped on someone . . . the girl chasing Chantel . . . the wraith must have got her," said Holly.

There was a horrified silence.

Adam fidgeted uneasily. He felt weird. His body was tingling as though he needed to run around and shake out excess energy. Swinging his legs under the table, he attempted to stop the tingles. It didn't work. If only Owen would decide upon a plan of action so there was no more waiting. If something didn't happen soon he felt as though he would explode.

Owen jumped up. He'd spotted a bat flying around the corner of the barn. "Swoop?" he called.

The bat circled above his head, squeaking in short sharp bursts.

The other children watched in amazement.

"You understand that?" asked Adam. His voice was full of disbelief.

"Sort of," said Owen. His eyes filled with tears. "They can't get Ava out. She's dying." He sat down at the table and buried his head in his arms.

"What are we going to do?" whispered Chantel.

No one answered. They stared at the locked-up barn.

Chantel squeezed her eyes shut. *Equus,* she called. She focused, sending the mindspeak with every ounce of her being. Her small body trembled with effort. She waited and waited for a reply. No waves of comfort washed over her, only her own despair.

Adam watched his little sister, a curl to his lip. He knew what she was doing, trying to save the universe again. Well, maybe she was out of luck. Maybe the Wise Ones weren't so wise after all.

Chantel finally looked across at him. Her big green eyes were so full of fear, his heart melted. He thrust out his hand and grasped hers.

"Adam," she said forlornly, "Equus isn't there."

Adam opened his mouth to comfort her when the tingling overtook his body. His mind was zapped by a slab of mindspeak so gigantic that it sounded as though someone was shouting.

CHILD, OPEN YOUR HEART AND HEAR ME! GO TO THE CIRCLE. YOU MUST ALL USE EARTH MAGIC TO WILL AVA BACK TO HER CIRCLE.

There was no mistaking the roar. It was Myrddin's voice.

Adam leaped to his feet. A Wise One had spoken to him! His face transformed. "Come on," he yelled. "Myrddin's sent me a message. We go to the Circle."

The urgency in Adam's voice drew everyone after him. Adam took off at a run across the courtyard.

"Wait for me," called Chantel.

Her brother stopped dead in his tracks. He changed direction and ran across to the Bath chair. "Get in quick."

Owen dashed his hand across his eyes and ran to help Adam push. Holly grabbed her bike and followed.

They hurried down the path, between the stones and into the center of the Great Circle.

"We have to make a circle," said Adam.

The tone of his voice stopped any arguing. Chantel climbed out of the Bath chair and the four of them joined hands.

"We have to do Earth Magic. We have to wish Ava here, will her to come back to her Circle."

The children looked helplessly at each other.

"It was in your dream, Owen, remember?" said Adam impatiently. "The people called Ava to the Circle. You described it."

"They had a rhyme, then they chanted her name," Owen said slowly. A glimmer of hope stirred in his heart. "They took a vow with the shaman." He paused, gathered his thoughts, then slowly recited. "'We all bear witness. Reveal and die. Let the Circle keep its secret while stones stand and hawks fly.' Then everyone began to chant her name, 'Ava, Ava, AVA, AVA'"

"Okay," said Adam, "let's do it. Now!"

"We all bear witness. Reveal and die. Let the Circle keep its secret while stones stand and hawks fly. Ava, Ava, Ava, Ava, Ava, Ava, Ava, Ava."

The four voices tailed off.

Holly looked around the field, embarrassed, but no one was watching their odd behavior. "I feel stupid," she admitted.

"I guess we have to believe it if it's going to work," said Owen uncertainly. "The people in my dream did. They really shouted out her name."

The cousins held hands again.

"Wish harder," exhorted Adam.

"Hurry up and make it work. Ava's dying." Owen squeezed the hands on either side of him. "She's dying on her own in the barn and there's no way we can get in." His voice grew and strengthened. "Earth Magic is what the people who built this Circle used. I saw it work." He stared around at the stones. "Adam's right. We have to really wish Ava here. We don't just say her name. We *will* her here with every bone in our bodies."

"When I call Equus, I close my eyes and see him in my head," said Chantel.

Holly smiled at her. "Good idea. We'll all try to see Ava as we chant her name."

Adam looked around the circle. "Ready? Now!"

The four children spoke together.

"We all bear witness. Reveal and die. Let the Circle keep its secret while stones stand and hawks fly. Ava, Ava, Ava, Ava, Ava, Ava, Ava, Ava."

The chant grew.

The children's eyes were closed and they swayed gently as they called more loudly. "AVA, AVA, AVA, AVA, AVA, AVA, AVA!"

A gentle swirl of wind stirred the children's hair as it spun in the center of their small circle. The children opened their eyes.

A hawk lay on the grass at their feet, blood seeping through the matted feathers at her breast.

Owen cried out. He fell to his knees and cradled Ava in his arms. Her head lolled. Her eyes were closed. He looked up at the others, his face white and full of dread.

Waiting for sunset was a nightmare. The children hid Ava in the Bath chair while they went in for tea, but no one ate much.

One by one they slipped out to check on the hawk as she lay panting on the cushion. Each time her body seemed smaller, flatter, as if life were oozing away. They covered her, dripped a little water into her beak, but nothing seemed to help.

Finally, the sun was an orange ball hanging near the horizon.

It was time.

Chantel waved them off.

The black silhouette of Silbury Hill loomed against the vivid sky. Holly, Owen and Adam jogged swiftly up the path and came out unnoticed behind the hill.

Holly ran to check the car park. All was clear.

"Now what? It better be quick!" said Owen, a catch in his voice. "I'm not sure Ava's breathing."

They peered at the bird cradled in his arms. Her eyelids flickered. Owen gave a tiny sob of relief.

"Here." Holly yanked on the wire fence and lifted it as high as she could. "Give Ava to Adam and crawl underneath."

Owen wriggled through to the other side of the fence. The sunset was fiercely orange, but he stood in the shadow of the hill and waited. Adam handed Ava over the fence. Then he and Holly helped each other through.

"I don't know what to do," said Owen.

"What if we circle seven times around the base of the hill?" said Adam. "That's what Chantel did when she raised the White Horse. We'll call for King Sel as we go round."

"Go, go, go." Holly's voice was urgent. "The sun's dropping fast."

Owen stepped into the glow of the sunset and stretched out his arms, offering Ava's body to the light, but her head hung slackly over the edge of his palm. Her eyes were shut and Owen could detect no breath. Tears rolled down his cheeks. He drew his arms back, laid her head against his shoulder and cradled her over his heart.

Holly's and Adam's voices rose around him.

"King Sel, please help us. Please help us, King Sel."

They trudged around the base of the hill seven times.

The sun touched the horizon and vivid beams shot across the shadowy landscape. One caught and held Owen in its spotlight.

Instinctively, he closed his eyes, threw back his head and shouted at the top of his lungs, "Hear me, King Sel. The Wise Ones need your help. I bring you Ava."

"Who calls the Golden King?" rumbled a voice that

seemed to echo from the center of the mound.

Adam nudged Holly. "We do, Holly and Adam!" they replied shakily.

"And me. I'm Owen." Owen opened his eyes fearfully. He sensed a movement behind him.

A shimmering light glowed in the shadows at the base of Silbury Hill. Within it was the faint form of a crowned king mounted on a horse. The horse started to circle the hill, gradually moving upward on a spiral path. The ghostly figures passed by the children without a sound, without acknowledgement.

Owen, Holly and Adam crept silently after them.

Round and round they spiraled, into the shadows and back to the light, climbing higher and higher. After each circuit the gold figures ahead grew more substantial.

It was a struggle. The hill was steep and the grass slippery. Owen could only steady himself with one hand for he held Ava tenderly with the other.

He scrabbled and scraped, lurching sideways and often slipping. His heart pounded. The spiral walk was taking forever, and the sun was sinking lower and lower.

Finally they reached the summit.

The horse and king paused. Caught in the last beam of sunlight, their every feature gleamed. The rippling muscles of the horse and each silky hair of his tail and mane could be counted. The golden rings of the king's finely wrought chain mail glittered and danced, and his shield was a blaze of reflected fire.

Holly and Adam fell to their knees and covered their eyes.

Only Owen remained standing. His knees trembled, but he met the king's stern gaze, Ava clutched to his heart.

The Golden King sat on his golden horse and looked down at the awestruck children.

"A Magic Child!" said the king. A brief smile crossed his features. He beckoned Owen forward.

Owen stumbled across the summit, half-blinded by the brilliance, half-blinded by tears. "It's too late." His voice was empty. "She's dead."

The Golden King bent forward and held out his shield.

Owen laid Ava in the hollow.

The Golden King supported the shield with one hand and slapped the reins with the other. His horse reared in salute, then cantered off the edge of the hill along the last golden beam of sunlight to the horizon.

FLASH! They vanished with the sun.

His heart breaking, Owen stared and stared after them.

The orange sky faded to pink, the pink to gray, and finally, when the gray matched the darkness in their hearts, the children crept home.

10.
EVERYBODY SWING

The darkness swirled, tossing Equus like a leaf in a storm. He struggled to keep upright, but the blackness was so complete that there was neither up nor down.

Screams of fury rang in his ears. "I sense you, Equus. You cannot hide forever." The Dark Being sent another wave of buffeting blackness followed by a vortex of sucking despair. It whirled randomly across the heavens as far as her range extended.

I have misjudged her strength, thought Equus. He struggled to fight the vortex, but despair clutched his heart and began to empty it of hope. Grimly, he held his head high. The talisman glinted. I hold the gold talisman. I hold the light, he told himself. I must keep the flame alive. He forced his muscles to fight the buffeting, to gallop from the clutching shadows.

Much, much later, Equus lay trembling with exhaustion be-

tween the shattered portals of the Gates of Sunrise. Though the great entrance to the Silver Citadel lay in ruins, and the Place Beyond Morning had been abandoned, he still found refuge there. Despite the onslaught of the Dark Being, invisible remnants of the Citadel's power hung in the air. Equus closed his eyes and let the remnants drift over his body. They caressed and refreshed him as only the healing powers of his home could.

He had courted annihilation and played mind games with the Dark Being. Mind games she had nearly won!

Equus shuddered at the memory of her strength. The balance of power had truly shifted. He would carry back to the Wise Ones knowledge of what he had feared. The Dark Being had gained enough strength to challenge them all.

A song roused him. A tiny bird, a lark, flew over the blackened walls of the Citadel and sang a welcome.

Equus raised his head.

The music washed over him, cleansing his spirit. With its help, Equus forced the dark memories deep into the recesses of his mind, to be pulled out and dealt with one by one with the wisdom of Myrddin and Ava.

Strengthened, Equus rose to his feet. "Little lark," he said, "you are the smallest of the inhabitants that fled the Place Beyond Morning, yet you are the first one back. Why?"

The lark paused in its song and tipped its head on one side. "You have found Magic Children," she answered, "and the shadow lightened."

Equus looked sadly across the ruins toward the mist hanging over the land he loved. "The shadow has deepened again."

"Every time I sing, it thins," replied the lark and opened

its throat. Out spilled a trill so beautiful, the air shimmered with light and the edge of the mist retreated.

Gladness filled Equus. "You are right, little lark. You shame me. The shadow has no power over true innocence. We shall both sing away the dark and welcome back the light."

Equus threw back his head and sang with the bird. His deep voice expressed his fears and sang of his desires. His voice roared in defiance and sweetened with hope, and the little lark trilled its song around his.

Finally the song was ended. With renewed heart and mind, Equus leaped for the stars and rode the winds toward Gaia.

Holly tiptoed past Owen's bed, bent over Adam and shook his shoulder.

He grunted.

She held a warning hand gently over his mouth. "Shhhhhh." She placed her lips nearer his ear. "Adam, it's time to go and save the Mother Tree. The rally's this morning."

Adam's eyes flickered and he frowned. He sat up looking rumpled and distressed. "I've hardly slept."

Holly sighed. "Me too." She squared her shoulders. "We couldn't stop Ava dying, but I'm not going to let the Mother Tree be destroyed. Are you coming or not?" she finished in a fierce whisper.

"I'm coming." Adam looked across at Owen, curled in a tight unhappy ball. "It's not going to be much fun around here." He rolled out of bed.

The two cousins pedaled one behind the other down the sunlit road. It was still before seven, and though the birds had been singing for hours, only a few cars passed them. The morning light was so bright that the world looked newly polished, and the wind in their faces smelled clean and fresh. Their spirits lightened.

Adam pumped his legs faster and drew level with Holly. "What's your plan?" he yelled.

Holly flashed him a grin. "A 'sit-in' up the tree."

Adam laughed. "Oh boy! For how long?"

"As long as it takes," said Holly firmly.

Chantel pushed her cereal around her plate.

"Are you feeling all right?" asked Aunt Lynne.

Chantel smiled weakly. "I'm fine. Just not very hungry."

"There's something going on again, isn't there?" Lynne's sudden attack caught Chantel by surprise. "It's not like Owen to sleep in late," she continued. "And where are Adam and Holly?"

"They've g . . . g . . . gone for a bike ride," muttered Chantel. She fingered the note in the pocket of her shorts. She'd promised Holly she'd leave it somewhere for Auntie Lynne to find. But it was still too early. Holly had insisted not before nine o'clock. "I don't want Dad driving down the highway to pick us up," she'd said. "So wait!"

Chantel waited, checking the clock every five minutes.

"How could they go off without telling us?" Lynne tutted crossly. "Holly certainly knows better than that!"

Chantel felt guiltier and guiltier. She wandered into the

kitchen and washed her dishes, then took refuge in the bed-room.

Despite the sunshine, Owen huddled under the bedcovers. He didn't care if he lived or died. Ava was dead. The knowledge carved a deep hole inside him, a hole as big as the universe. He wished he could fall through it to oblivion.

The church clock struck nine.

"Finally," sighed Chantel with relief. She straightened her bed, turned and stuck the note between the pillow and rumpled quilt of Holly's unmade bed. Auntie Lynne would be sure to come in and fix it.

She reentered the kitchen. "Can I go read in the Stone Circle?" she asked.

Lynne nodded. "If you see Holly and Adam, tell them I want to speak to them."

"Okay," said Chantel uncomfortably. She limped out as fast as she could.

Holly and Adam hid their bikes among the ferns and crept through Savernake Forest.

Though they had made good time, they were far from the first protesters there. Over fifty people had gathered. Some hung around in the car park and others were striding determinedly along the road toward a parked yellow bull-dozer in a lay-by.

"Darn," said Holly, spying out the land from behind a bush. "I was hoping we'd be here first. We need to get up the tree without anyone seeing us."

"No one is in the forest," pointed out Adam. "They're too busy discussing chaining up the bulldozer."

"Good. Let's go to the Mother Tree before they notice us."

Holly dropped to her hands and knees and began to crawl through the bracken. Adam followed. The journey was rough and uncomfortable and they were scratched and covered with burrs and grass stains by the time they reached the edge of the Mother Tree's thick tangle of roots.

"Stay here," whispered Holly. "I'll find out what's going on."

She disappeared into the bracken again.

Adam gazed in awe at the twisted black trunk ahead. "Holly was right, you really are old!"

Holly crawled to the edge of the high bank and peeked over.

A sea of heads, some bald, some with flowing curls, some sporting hats, caps and head scarves, milled around on the road below. Snatches of conversations floated up.

" . . . take it in turns to lie in front of the bulldozer."

" . . . I don't agree. No chains. No vandalizing."

" . . . remember . . . peaceful protest."

A police car edged its way up the road and parked behind the bulldozer. The crowd turned to watch and a scatter of boo's were heard.

Holly withdrew and crawled back to Adam. "Everyone's busy. Let's climb the tree." She stood up, clambered over the roots and swung herself up into the branches.

Adam followed.

<hr>

Chantel sat with her back against one of the stones, her nose buried in her book. A shadow fell across the pages. She looked up.

"Mum found the note," said Owen. "She's on the cell phone to Dad."

Chantel sighed. She moved over.

Owen flung himself down. "It was awful, Chantel. I don't know what to do."

"Me neither," whispered Chantel. She knew he wasn't referring to Holly or Adam. "Equus won't answer. What if something's happened to him too?"

They looked at each other with haunted eyes.

<hr>

Adam and Holly straddled a large branch within the umbrella of green leaves. Adam's eyes were wide. He pointed to the mistletoe.

Holly nodded. She leaned forward and stroked the trunk. "Hello, Tree," she whispered. "We've come to help."

"I bid you welcome, young Holly Berry." The tree's voice was a faint rustle. "You bring a friend?"

"My cousin, Adam."

"Welcome, Adam." A green leaf brushed his cheek.

"Er . . . thanks." Adam shifted on the branch. This was getting awfully weird.

"I've lots to tell you," Holly whispered, her mouth close to the tree bark, "but I don't want anyone to hear."

"Mindspeak," whispered the tree.

Holly made herself comfortable. She leaned her back against the main trunk and closed her eyes, organizing her thoughts to tell the tale of the acorn, the wraith and Ava's death.

Adam watched, torn between embarrassment and envy.

"Now, now, what's going on 'ere then?" The policeman, accompanied by a workman in overalls, strolled down the road toward the group of protesters.

"You knows as well as I, Dan Pierce. It's bin in all the papers," retorted one of the protesters.

The policeman grinned. "I 'ave to ask though, don't I, William Blythe? You might all just be passing through. Taking a walk like."

"I'll tell you what ain't taking a walk. That there bulldozer," shouted someone from the back of the crowd.

"Is that so?" The policeman leaned casually against the offending machine. "Now, why's that?"

"Because we're going to stop it, that's why!" shouted a woman waving a placard declaring *TREES YES! ROADS NO! COUNTY COUNCIL GOT 2 GO!*

She pushed her way to the front of the crowd and waggled the placard in the policeman's face.

He gently moved it aside.

"Oh, give over, Daniel Pierce. You don't like the clearing of the old trees any better than us. Your missis signed the petition," said the man called William Blythe.

"That's as may be, but my job's the law." The policeman surveyed the crowd and spoke slowly and clearly. "You all have a right to protest. Freedom of speech, we call it. But you are required to stand on the side of the road and allow other citizens to pass by."

The protesters made a line along the road.

"And Doug Metcalfe here has a right to go to his place of work."

The man in overalls climbed into the cab of the bulldozer accompanied by shouts of derision. He switched it on. Several people from the crowd moved to stand in front of the bulldozer's blade. Doug switched it off, sat back and took a pack of sandwiches from his pocket.

The policeman nodded his approval. "Now that's what I call a civilized protest. Remember, don't block the road. I reckon there'll be some right interesting citizens passing by."

The crowd laughed.

"I'll be watching from my car as requested. Call if you need me. Morning all." The policeman strolled back up the road.

The man in the bulldozer offered a sandwich to the nearest protester.

Adam nearly fell out of the tree. "Did you see that, Holly? And the cop? Are they all like that over here? Where's his gun?"

143

Holly opened her eyes. "Give me a break. He doesn't need one. He knows everyone." She sat upright. "What's that?"

A series of ominous rhythmic bangs came closer and closer. Both children lay along the branch and peered through the leaves. A contingent of riot troops, rhythmically pounding their shields, marched up the road. A roar of disbelief rose from the protesters.

<hr />

Deep in the forest, the wild boar stirred restlessly. His peaceful refuge was invaded. The hated human smell hung strong in the air around him. He snuffled and grunted, his tiny eyes darting angrily toward anything that moved.

A dead branch trembled in a fitful breeze.

The boar charged, trampled and gored until the branch lay in smithereens. He stood over the pieces, sniffing uneasily.

Then the banging started.

<hr />

Adam clutched Holly's arm. "Who's declared war?" He stared down in horror at the advance of armored men. "This only happens in movies . . . Why are they here? No one's done anything bad."

A stunned Holly shook her head.

In perfect rhythm the riot troops marched up the road and made a line below the tree, their featureless masks facing the protesters.

There was a deadly silence.

The protesters inched back. They had no stomach for this. Protesting the cutting of an ancient forest was one thing, but facing riot troops was another.

"AT EASE," roared a voice. The troops relaxed their stance and pushed up their helmets to show the sweaty faces of the local constabulary.

There were angry shouts from the protesters and a surge forward.

The troop captain stepped out, his hand up.

"HOLD IT," he roared.

Everyone froze.

"Apologies if our outfits scared you. We're on a training exercise. Not too much chance to train for crowd control in this neck of the woods." He paused, waiting for a chuckle from the crowd.

The protesters stared stonily at him.

The troop captain cleared his throat. "So since we're required to attend your protest, we thought we'd kill two birds with one stone and save taxpayers' money."

Someone snorted derisively.

BOOM! BOOM! BOOM! An insistent drumbeat interrupted him.

An entire brass band marched up the road.

Oh when the protesters, come marching in, everyone sang at the top of their voices. *When the protesters come marching in.*

Oh I want to be in their number, when the protesters come marching in.

The trombonist gave an extra twiddle on his instrument as the band marched past the police car. The policeman double-tooted the horn in reply. The riot troops moved over to make room.

"I tell you, everyone in England's mad!" said Adam with conviction.

Holly laughed.

The wild boar was terrified. He could identify most forest noises, but these sounds he'd never heard before. They hurt his ears, and a strong human smell came with them. It was time to defend his home. Head down, he began to charge through the bracken toward the noise.

The delegate from the county council arrived in an official car, followed closely by the van from the local TV station. He stepped out, straightened his tie, smiled at the camera and launched into a prepared speech. "I would like to reassure you . . . "

"BOO! SHAME ON YOU!" shouted voices from the crowd.

" . . . that your county council is aware of the delicate balance between preservation of our natural areas and the need for progress . . . "

"THEN SAVE OUR TREES!" came the shouts while the band loudly played "We Shall Overcome."

With a squeal of rage, the wild boar erupted from the bracken and appeared at the top of the bank. The dirt overhang gave way beneath him. In a mini landslide, the boar slithered down and landed half-dazed in the middle of the road.

The troop captain acted instinctively. "Circle enemy!" he roared.

With a single movement the riot troops pushed their visors in place, lowered their shields to the ground and made an impenetrable wall around the confused boar.

The protesters applauded and the TV cameras rolled.

With a gesture of resignation the county councillor hauled out his cell phone and requested a vet and tranquilizer darts.

Holly stuck her head through the leaves. "So, are you going to call it quits now?" she called.

Everyone looked up.

"Who the heck are you?" called the councillor.

"Holly and Adam. We're doing a sit-in."

Adam's face appeared. "We're not coming down until you promise to save the trees."

Cheers and applause erupted.

The councillor groaned as the TV crew zoomed in. He'd been told never to compete for publicity with kids and dogs, and now he had kids and a wild boar. He was toast!

"I've researched a really good reason why you shouldn't cut the trees," called Holly. "And now there's another." She pointed down to the wild boar, which was trying to gore a hole in a riot shield. "That's a rare animal and this is its natural habitat. I think it should be protected."

"You're a smart kid," called out an approving voice.

A microphone was poked up toward Holly. "And what's this research you've done, young lady?" asked the grinning TV reporter.

"Well," said Holly, "my dad told me that Savernake Forest was a royal forest so I looked it up in the museum. It's still a royal forest. The ancient laws say a man can be hanged for cutting down trees without royal assent." Holly looked down at the councillor. "Did you ask the queen?" she inquired.

"I cannot answer that question without checking with council," he muttered as he slid into the back of his car. "Drive," he exhorted his chauffeur.

Doug Metcalfe checked the brakes on his bulldozer and climbed down from the cab. "I reckon my boss will want to wait to see if I'm liable to be hanged." He grinned and waved to the policeman. "Hey, Dan, going to give me a lift back?"

The band swung into a familiar tune.

"For she's a jolly good fellow," warbled the crowd.

❈❈❈

"Blessings," rustled the Mother Tree. "Holly, you have earned the mistletoe bough." She bent down the branch so Holly could snap it off.

"Hold out your hand, Adam."

Adam obeyed and an acorn dropped into his palm. "Thanks," he said.

"Use it against the wraith. Then bury it," instructed the Mother Tree. "And cleanse your mind of its wickedness. Earth Magic will not fail this time."

"And Ava and the Wise Ones?" asked Holly urgently. "Can you do anything to help them?"

"Dark and light," murmured the Mother Tree. "The dark is always blackest before the light shines again. Go in peace, young saplings. May your leaves be ever green."

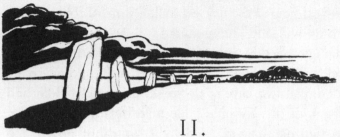

II.
THE DANCE OF THE STONES

The TV crew loaded the bikes in the rear of the van and drove Holly and Adam back to Avebury.

Lynne stood in the doorway, her nails tapping the door-frame. Holly and Adam exchanged a glance.

"Uh oh," whispered Adam.

The explanations and introductions were a little tense.

"We'd like to film an interview with Holly and Adam in the museum," the reporter explained to Lynne. "That's where Holly found the information about royal assent."

Lynne nodded shortly. "They'll be along in a minute." She watched while the TV crew left to set up its equipment, then turned and fixed a steely eye on the children. "As soon as the interview is completed, Holly, you and Adam meet with me in the kitchen. I'll be waiting." She turned to Owen and Chantel. "You come too." She entered the kitchen. The door swung to with a slight bang.

"I warned you," breathed Holly. "There'll be a row. We'll be grounded." She followed the TV crew toward the museum.

Chantel looked miserable. "I hate it when people scream."

"Oh, she won't scream," Holly said. "She goes all quiet and reasonable. It's worse!"

Owen thumped the nearest wall. "None of this has anything to do with me," he muttered.

Adam grabbed his arm. "Owen." He looked around for Chantel and beckoned her over. "If we're going to be grounded, you two have to do something quick. Holly and I will be with the TV crew." He held out the new acorn. "Go to the manor gardens, say the words of power and throw this at the thing that was after Chantel," he whispered rapidly. "When it's an acorn again, bury it. That's what the Mother Tree said to do."

Owen shook his head. "Not me. Forget it."

Chantel bit her lip. "I'm not going on my own. What if something goes wrong?"

"Hurry up, Adam," called Holly from the open doorway.

Adam glared at Owen. "You have to! We've got to capture the wraith again and set the girl free. She's already been there overnight. We don't want more trouble."

"All right, all right, if Mum will let us out of the house. But count me out after this." Owen grabbed the acorn. "I'm doing nothing more. Get it? NOTHING!" He poked his head into the kitchen and tried to sound less angry. "Mum, can Chantel and I go and watch if we promise to come back with Holly and Adam?"

Lynne sighed. "Can I trust you?"

"It wasn't us that took off!" said Owen, carefully avoiding the issue.

"I suppose." Lynne pushed her hair back uneasily. "But come straight back."

Owen and Chantel pushed through the turnstile and made their way toward the topiary garden.

Chantel poked Owen warningly.

A young woman and an older man, both in coveralls and green Wellington boots, were standing beside the ivy figure in the middle of the path.

The man scratched his head. "It's a right old mystery. Lord Mayerthorpe knows nothing about it."

"It's very realistic," remarked the woman. She tried to stick her hand through the ivy. "It must be on a wire frame." She tried to waggle the sculpture. "The foundation's strong."

The children watched while both gardeners tried to heave the ivy figure up from the path. They had no success.

"We're going to have to cut it down," panted the woman. "Pity."

The man shook his head. "There doesn't seem much point in an elaborate joke like this. Wonder who did it."

The woman shrugged. "We'll need wire cutters as well as the pruning shears." They passed the children with barely a nod.

"Quick, let's get this over before they come back." Owen pulled the acorn from his pocket.

Chantel limped after him.

"Ready?" asked Owen. "I throw, you say the words. Then we grab the acorn and beat it!"

"I'm ready." Chantel's voice quavered.

Owen flung the acorn.

"Lhiat myr hoilloo," shouted Chantel.

The acorn hit the ivy figure, shattered, and green light flickered and jumped from leaf to leaf like electricity. With a sigh, the ivy fell in a heap around the feet of the dazed girl. A faint smudge of mist left her mouth. The acorn fragments gathered around it and re-formed. Owen shot out his hand and snatched the acorn before it could fall to the ground.

"Run, before she comes to," he muttered and spun away.

Chantel hobbled after him. "Wow. Is that what happened to me?"

Owen ignored her. He rushed through the manor grounds and popped out of the exit like a cork from a bottle. Grabbing the Bath chair, he jiggled impatiently until Chantel caught up with him.

They were on their way to the museum when they heard a terrified yell from the gardens.

"Help, someone! I've been abducted by aliens."

⁂

The meeting with Lynne was not as bad as the children expected. It was hard for her to be angry when Holly and Adam were being hailed as heroes. However, all four children were grounded for the rest of the day, despite protests from Owen.

"Oh, Owen, stop moaning," Holly finally snapped as they sprawled on the back lawn reading. "We're all in this together."

"Yes, but I'm the one who's stuck with the stupid wraith in my pocket," snapped back Owen.

"Oh no!" groaned Adam. "I told you to bury it."

"And when was I supposed to do that?" said Owen sarcastically. "We couldn't hang around in the garden, then we had to boot it back and get grounded with you two."

"Take it out of your pocket," said Holly sharply. "What if you sit on it and it smashes?"

"Exactly!" said Owen. He pulled out the acorn. "So, do we bury it here? The Circle would be safer."

"We *are* inside the Circle, idiot. The stones are all around us, remember?"

"I know, but does the garden count as much as being in the field beside a stone?"

"It counts," said Holly softly. "The whole area has been a special place for thousands of years. Yes, it counts."

Owen held out the acorn to Holly. "You bury it."

Holly stuck her hands on her hips. "Owen Maxwell, smarten up! You're the chosen one this time. It's up to you. Are you going to give up, chicken out and let the Dark Being get the circlet? Or are you going to organize Ava's ritual? We can bury the acorn at the same time."

For a moment Owen rocked on the balls of his feet as though he were going to launch himself in fury at Holly. Instead, he took a deep breath. "The ritual," he said clearly.

Owen lay on his back on his bed, staring at the ceiling. He still had not figured out what to do and twilight was approaching fast.

The loss of Ava haunted him, but now his grief was tempered with determination. He was going to find her circlet and hand it over to the remaining Wise Ones as she had requested. Just how to do it eluded him. Desperately he went over and over the dreams, trying to decide on the key bits. If only Ava could help. Tears gathered in his eyes. He dashed them away. If only the stones could talk. Hey . . . the stones!

Owen leaped to his feet and slipped down the stairs. He paused as he passed the living room. The TV was on. Good, everyone else was in there. He slipped out the kitchen door.

Keeping to the shadows, Owen ran silently down the garden and through the gate to the nearest stone. He threw his arms around it and laid his cheek on the surface.

At first there was nothing. He made himself relax. Then it happened. He heard and felt the slow steady heartbeat.

"Stone," he whispered, "please help me. How do I find Ava's circlet? What do I have to do to make you dance?"

A ripple of amusement ran through the stone. *Magic Child, we thought you'd never think to ask. Listen and learn, listen and learn.*

Owen closed his eyes and concentrated. His heartbeat slowed and beat as one with the heart of the stone. Images flew through his mind, ancient words whispered in his ears and strength flowed from the stone into his heart.

Finally Owen stood. "Thank you," he said formally and bowed to the stone. "I think I understand." Swift as a hawk he flew back to the house and slipped upstairs to his room.

No one had missed him.

It was midnight. The moon was full. Brittle white light washed across Gaia, illuminating the stones and the sleeping village.

Equus and Myrddin gazed down at the peaceful scene in silence. They, and the universe, held their breath.

Small shadows moved! Four children crept from a darkened cottage and made their way across the village street, through the stile, to the far side of the Stone Circle.

The Wise Ones waited.

"If only we could . . . " began Equus.

Myrddin stretched out a warning hand. "Trust. They must find their own way to express what's in their hearts."

Equus fell silent again.

A tiny orange light flickered, then another, and another, many small candles making a circle. A circle within the Circle, one not easily seen from the village, but one that could be seen from the stars.

Myrddin and Equus exchanged hopeful glances.

Suddenly Myrddin raised his arms. "Blessings," he roared. "Owen has chosen well. This is the magic night Ava was waiting for. Look at her stones!"

"Oh, look at the stones." Chantel unconsciously echoed the Wise Ones.

The other children, sitting on the ground within the circle of candles, looked up.

Each stone glowed.

"Listen." Holly tilted her head.

"It's their heartbeats." Owen's voice was filled with awe as he identified the deep pulse in the air. "We're doing it right." He straightened his body and visibly gained in stature and confidence. He gently touched five objects lying in the

155

middle of the circle: a lump of earth, a feather, a candle, a bucket of water and the mistletoe. "The stones said the earth, water, fire and air are symbols to help our minds focus. It doesn't matter how we use them, and that's why everyone's ritual is different. As long as we concentrate and believe." Owen bent forward and picked up the hawk's feather that he had found the first day. "The symbol of the air we breathe. It reminds me of Ava and makes her seem closer."

Holly stretched out her hand and picked up the lump of soil. She crumbled it and let the dust drop back to the ground. "Earth supports us and strengthens us." She broke a sprig of mistletoe from the bough in front of her and tucked it in the buttonhole of her shirt. "And the plant that needs no earth reminds me of all the wonders and mysteries we will never be able to explain."

Adam touched the bucket of water. "Water from the stream that doesn't run. Without water, things die. It also cleans us. This reminds us to clean our hearts as well as our bodies." He plunged in his hand and shook drops over everyone.

Chantel lit a candle in a small holder. She held it up. "Fire gives us warmth and makes a light in the darkness. It stops us being scared." She placed the candle in the middle of their circle and stretched out her arms.

The children clasped their hands to complete a third circle with the flame at its heart. "A circle of children," said Holly, "within a circle of fire, within the Great Circle of Stones. Let's try the chant now."

"Light and Dark, Dark and Light," said the children softly.

Light and Dark, Dark and Light, joined in Equus and Myrddin.

Light and Dark, Dark and Light, called out a strong new voice.

> *Sun by day, Moon by night,*
> *Man and woman, adult, child,*
> *Bird and beast, both tame and wild,*
> *Past and present, far and near,*
> *Patience, anger, hope and fear,*
> *Frantic movement, contemplation . . .*

Dave the Druid materialized in the shadows beyond the candles. *The Dance of Stones, a celebration*! he finished. He smiled at the children. "You called us all. Come, join the dance." He held out his hands.

As in a dream and without fear, the children stepped over the circle of fire and joined the shadow people within the Great Circle of Stones.

Owen recognized figures from the past: the two shamans, the People of the Deer and the People of the Hawk, Hewll and Ulwin and their families, even the men and women from the night of destruction. Chantel and Holly recognized people from the naming ceremony: the woman with the baby, the drummers and dancers, even the teenage girl. There were many other shadow people no one knew.

Adam tried to understand. "Who are they? Are they ghosts? Are we dead?"

"No, we are joining the memories of all those who are, and have ever been, part of the great Circle Dance," replied Dave the Druid. "Are you ready? It's beginning."

A line formed and the shadow people began to wind in

and out between the stones. The children and Dave joined in as the line passed by. Each stone's light pulsed. *BOOM! BOOM! BOOM!* thudded the heartbeat. It was all around, in front, behind, in the air above and vibrating from the ground below.

The line stepped in time, winding around stone after stone.

Owen turned his head. "The missing stones are back," he whispered, for as they danced past each gap, up rose a ghost stone.

Round and round stepped the line again, in and out of the ghost stones as well as the real stones until the Great Circle was complete.

The heartbeat quickened. The dance steps matched it. Dancers held hands and made their circle within the Stone Circle. They circle danced for the sun, with the glow from the candles' flames on their faces.

Next the dancers turned outward and faced toward the stones. They danced for the moon and stars, bathed in the pulsing white light.

Finally they danced for the stones themselves. Faster and faster the dancers stepped until each stone spun on its axis in a swirl of sound and light.

"The stones, they dance!" Owen cried.

Time and space met.

The village faded away, the great white walls of chalk from the ditch rose protectively around the Stone Circle, and beyond the ditch spread the ancient forest of sacred oaks.

KER-BOOM! KER-BOOM! KER-BOOM! KER-BOOM!
The heartbeat slowed and stopped. Everyone turned silently

to the center of the Circle where the children's candles glowed with orange flames.

The hawk-headed shaman beckoned to Hewll. Antler pick in hand, Hewll strode into the center and thrust the pick into the ground, peeling back turf and exposing a small slab of rock. Hewll beckoned to the children. They circled the slab and stared at it.

Everyone watched.

Owen took Hewll's pick. He tried to pry up the rock slab. It was immovable. All four children crouched and thrust their fingers into the cracks around the edge. They pulled together. Nothing moved.

"Earth Magic hid the circlet. Only Earth Magic can reveal it," whispered Dave the Druid.

"I don't know what else to do," Owen cried.

"Think of your dreams. The clue must be in your dreams," said Holly. "Think."

Owen thought. He relived everything he'd seen in the circle dreams. Nothing.

"Come on, Owen. There must be something that you haven't tried."

Owen shook his head. "Only breaking the stone." He looked at the other kids. "Hey, maybe that's it! Ava showed me the night of destruction. The stones were broken by the blacksmith. We need wood and fire and water." He turned to the gathering behind him.

Each shaman through the ages lifted one arm and held up a stick.

Owen pointed to Holly. "Place the mistletoe ball over the slab."

Holly dropped it in place.

"Stack the sticks on top," Owen shouted, and one by one the shamans from the past moved silently forward and built a small bonfire.

Owen pointed to Chantel. "You are the bringer of fire."

Chantel picked up a candle, held the flame to a stick and stepped back.

All eyes watched.

The tiny flame flickered and glowed and licked the end of a second stick. That too began to flicker. Both flames danced and spread, until with a crackle and roar a small bonfire lit up the night sky and the onlookers' faces.

Owen waited until the fire died down and the coals at its heart glowed red and hot.

He pointed to Adam. "Now!" he shouted. "Water from the stream that does not run."

Adam picked up the bucket and dashed the ice-cold water on the fire. There was a hiss and a loud *CRACK*, followed by an acrid stench and billows of smoke. The children covered smarting eyes and coughed and choked.

"Did it work?" gasped Adam.

Owen was too busy coughing to answer. He waited until the smoke had cleared, then, using Hewll's pick, he raked the coals to one side.

The rock slab had split across its middle. Owen stretched out his hands to lift the slab.

"Careful, it's hot," warned Holly.

"It isn't. It's Earth Magic," said Owen. He lifted aside the two pieces of rock, thrust his hand in the cavity and brought out a small pot.

A sigh like the rustle of autumn leaves rippled through the watchers. The chief shaman, her golden mask glinting in the candlelight, glided to the center and stood before Owen.

He handed her the pot. With reverence, she lifted the lid, pulled out the leather bag and offered it to Owen. Hand trembling, Owen removed the circlet and held it high.

"Ava, Ava, Ava, AVA," the ghostly whispers rose as the shadow dancers knelt.

"Should we kneel?" whispered Holly.

Owen shook his head. "We are Magic Children. We have a journey to take." He turned toward the entrance to the Avenue.

King Sel and his golden horse stood waiting. The king raised a finger and beckoned. Owen approached. Holly, Adam and Chantel followed. One by one, King Sel lifted the children and placed them on Aurora's broad back. They sat astride, holding tightly to the waist of the child before. Owen sat at the front holding Ava's circlet.

The king twitched the reins and Aurora stepped forward. He led the way along the moonlit Avenue that wound serpent-like across the land toward the Sanctuary. Dave the Druid fell in behind. Behind him processed the many shamans from the past. The dancers followed.

Tears of joy ran unchecked down Myrddin's face. "Light and Dark, Dark and Light. The followers of light gather, despite threatening darkness."

"They gather because darkness threatens," said Equus gently. He stamped his hoof and sent a shower of shooting *stars toward Gaia.* "My talisman is regained, and Ava's circlet is within reach. The Mother Tree speaks and the Forest Magic is rekindled. You are right, Myrddin, the Old Magic is strengthening. If only the children can keep light in their hearts, soon we will rejoice."

The procession wound its solemn way toward a small round wooden building on a cleared hill.

"Enter the Sanctuary," said King Sel as the Avenue emerged from the forest. "The last steps of the journey you must take alone."

One by one he lifted the children down and pointed toward the building.

The children stepped hesitantly onto velvet-smooth grass inside a circle of living oak trees. In the center loomed the Sanctuary. There were no windows and there was no door, only a black opening between upright posts.

Chantel slid her hand into Adam's. He grasped it tightly.

Holly stepped closer to Owen. "I don't like this," she whispered.

"Me neither," Owen admitted. He turned back to King Sel.

The Golden King sat on his horse, blocking the return down the Avenue. Dave the Druid and the other shamans stood between the encircling oak trees. Their faces were kindly but unyielding. There was no way back.

The Golden King raised his arm and pointed sternly to the black opening.

"Enter you must, but remember the light."

Hand in hand the two pairs of children stepped through the doorway. There was only one way to turn, down a narrow passage of wattle walls that pressed against them. It forced them to wind around and around farther into the dark. Owen and Holly went first.

The blackness was full of voices.

Each child heard something different.

Owen heard Ava crying for help. Her voice echoed and re-echoed in his head. Then came the visions. He relived her bleeding to death in his arms. Sobs shook his frame and the darkness around him entered his body. With each step came more black despair.

Holly heard laughing. Older girls were laughing at her. She hated people laughing at her, embarrassing her and making her feel small. Suddenly she heard the scornful voice of the long-haired girl telling Holly what a jerk she was. Holly knew she was useless. She trembled, knowing that even though she tried to be strong, it was no use. She would never be brave and clever and responsible like them. She would never achieve anything. The feelings of failure rolled over her and weighed her down. What was the point of going on?

Adam heard his father and mother. His parents' voices were raised in anger, screaming that they were divorcing because of him. Adam cowered against the wall. He'd known it all along. Everything *was* his fault. They were right. He was a nasty horrible person; he had no friends; he scared his sister; his cousins didn't want him; and he'd made his parents fight. Adam felt his heart breaking.

Chantel huddled at his side. She too heard her parents shouting. She hated shouting. Trembling, she tried to shut out the cruel words by placing her hands over her ears, but the words were inside her head . . . Hateful words that got bigger and louder and whirled madly around her brain, driving out everything else. She was in their way. They didn't love her. That was why she was sent to England. She saw her mother throwing her clothes in a suitcase and thrusting her roughly in the cab. With a moan, Chantel sank to the floor.

Owen's hand hurt as it tightened around the sharp edge of Ava's circlet. The hurt reminded him of the circlet, reminded him to think of light. He tried to remember why, and the darkness around his hand lightened. He lifted his hand and the stone in the circlet glowed.

"Remember the light," Owen yelled suddenly. "We have to remember the light." He held the circlet aloft so all the children could see the faint gleam.

The voices in his head lessened.

Owen concentrated on the stone; he remembered the silvery light in the Place Beyond Morning and his first sight of Ava, the magnificent half-woman, half-bird, whose magic encased and shimmered around her.

The despair in his heart eased as the stone shone.

"Keep the light in your heart," he called, though his voice trembled with the effort.

Holly's hand squeezed his. "It's a test, isn't it?" she whispered. "We have to be strong and believe in ourselves."

"I think so," Owen whispered back.

Holly made herself stand up straight and mentally look the older girls in the eye. Stop laughing, she told them. It's wrong to try to destroy people's confidence.

The laughter in her head faded and the light grew.

Owen half turned so the light fell behind him on Adam and Chantel. They were huddled together on the floor, Adam's arms over Chantel's body.

Owen held the circlet over them. "The light," he called. "Remember the light."

Adam struggled to surface through thoughts as thick and black as treacle. He grasped Chantel's hand and pulled her to her feet. "It's not our fault," he said. The light around him grew. He shook Chantel gently. "See them. Tell them. Say it with me. 'It's not our fault.'"

"It's not our fault," repeated Chantel dully. She opened tear-drenched eyes and saw the light growing around them. "Don't be mad at us, Mom," she whimpered. "We're just kids."

Adam threw back his head and roared at the top of his lungs, "MOM, DAD, DON'T YOU GET IT? IT'S NOT OUR FAULT!"

Despite the blackness, despite her terror, Chantel smiled.

The four children stumbled out of the dark into the Sanctuary's heart, a space open to the sky and flooded with moonlight.

They rubbed their eyes and held their hands and faces up to the stars. "Oh, how beautiful."

The hawk's body lay on the stone marking the center of the Sanctuary.

Owen froze. He nudged the others.

Joy left them.

They drew closer, forming a circle around the stone.

Owen stretched out one finger and stroked the hawk's head. He laid the circlet on her breast.

Stars danced, light shimmered. A mighty wind swirled and buffeted the children. They staggered back against the inner walls of the Sanctuary, hands over their eyes.

When the turmoil stopped they peeked through their fingers.

Ava, in full magnificence as half-hawk, half-woman, the circlet shining from her feathery hair, smiled down on them. "Magic Child and true friend! Owen, I thank you." She raised her wings and shone so brightly that Holly, Chantel and Adam turned their heads. Only Owen forced his eyes to meet her gaze.

Ava's voice rang out. "With courage and friendship you kept the light alive. You came through the darkness without me." A feathery touch from her wings brushed across each child's head. "Owen, Holly, Adam and Chantel, Magic Children all. You believe, therefore you succeed."

She flew toward the sky and circled the Sanctuary, trailing a rainbow of light from the edges of her wings. The light enfolded the children and lifted them to the stars. For one brief moment they glimpsed the Sanctuary far below. The dream people surrounding it gazed skyward in wonder. "AVA, AVA, AVA, AVA," came the distant shout.

WHOOSH, they were gone.

Owen, Holly, Chantel and Adam sat on the ground in the center of the Circle. They were stiff and cold. Chantel shivered.

Owen and Holly clambered to their feet. Adam rose and turned to help Chantel. They all stared around at the moonlit scene: the sleeping village of Avebury and the stones.

Owen kicked a melted candle stub and the small pile of black ash. "Did it happen or did we dream it?" he asked.

Everyone shrugged.

"We'd better go before anyone catches us," said Holly. She started across the field.

"Wait," said Chantel. "Look."

Her cast had caught the edge of a small, stone-lined hole. Beside it lay the split slab, an empty clay pot and a leather pouch.

Adam picked up the pouch and pot and handed them to Owen. "For you, I think!"

Owen felt in his pocket and pulled out the acorn. He dropped it in the pouch and tucked it in the pot. Bending, he replaced the pot in the cavity and carefully fitted the two pieces of rock slab back in place. Adam helped him kick ashes and dirt over the top.

"We'd better say the words of power," he murmured.

"Lhiat myr hoilloo," the four children whispered.

A haze of green spread and healed the scar.

"The stones danced, and my circlet is freely returned," rejoiced Ava. *"I am whole again."*

She lit up the heavens with her beauty.

Equus and Myrddin glowed with joy.

"The children's strength is amazing," said Equus. "None before have traveled the Sanctuary's dark without Ava's help."

"They survived because they were children. Their in-

167

ner demons were the demons of innocence," Ava said. "My rainbow light has given them comfort; they will remember being tempered, but have already forgotten the agony."

"When Owen lost you, Adam finally heard me." Myrddin raised his arms and shook out his cloak in delight. "That young man and I will have a fine seeking together."

"Have you asked them? Are the children still willing to further our quest?" asked Ava. "The recovery of my circlet was harder than we either hoped or intended. The dark influence on Gaia lurks in more than the woodlands around Avebury. The unlocking of your staff may not be so simple, Myrddin."

Myrddin nodded. "You are right, Ava. We must ask them." He closed his eyes and sent a mindspeak roaring through the stars.

Adam, hear me. Time is short. Will you help regain my staff?

Adam had drifted into an exhausted sleep. The mindspeak broke into his dreams.

Sure I'll help, Myrddin. But not now. I'm tired. Adam buried his head farther into his pillow. Deep and healing oblivion overtook him.

"Myrddin," rebuked Ava, "the children must recover."

Before Myrddin could reply, another voice roared through the heavens.

"I sense magic in the air, Wise Ones. Soon I will find you."

"The Dark Being," said Ava. She dimmed her light and the Wise Ones looked fearfully across the universe.

The approaching black cloud loomed larger.

Author's Note

Stone Circles have always been special places in my life. I played in one as a child. I would lie on my back at its heart and try to imagine the people who made it. I have visited many Stone Circles throughout the United Kingdom, including Stonehenge, but the Circle that made the greatest impact on me is Avebury.

Avebury is a people's Circle. A village has grown up within its stones; you can walk around them, pat them and picnic beside them. Ceremonies are held there, and while I am sure that they are different ceremonies from those devised by the builders of the Circle, they give a sense of continuity and familiarity that is missing from many prehistoric monuments. This Stone Circle is not just an amazing monument from the past; it is part of people's lives. People still tell stories about the stones. One is supposed to spin on its axis at midnight on New Year's Eve. Another has a ledge-like seat; if you sit on it, the devil is supposed to get you!

The setting of *Dance of the Stones* uses many features I discovered in the Avebury area. The Circle nestles in the heart of a massive area recognized as a "sacred landscape" by English Heritage. The area encompasses not only Avebury and Stonehenge, but also many other ancient sites including several important neolithic barrows, hill forts and puzzling Silbury Hill.

Dance of the Stones is a fantasy, as is my explanation of the name Avebury and my descriptions of the use of the

Circle. The raising of the final stone in the story happened purely in my imagination. I am not a historical scholar; however, I based it on my interpretation of clues I found in the Avebury museums. Archeologists uncovered a pile of antler picks and scapula shovels in the bottom of the great ditch. Why were they abandoned there? I give my own explanation. The characters of Hewll and Ulwin are based on what I understand of the latest interpretation of neolithic people. I set the raising of the stone in winter because I think people without many tools would harness the elements to help, and moving a monolith over frozen ground made sense to me, though it meant the pit would have to be prepared in summer or fall. As it would take some time to dig a pit with bone tools, again this made sense.

My description of the "night of destruction" is only loosely based on facts. There was indeed a man known as the Barber Surgeon who may have helped topple the stones. He was crushed when one fell on him. His remains were found by archeologists. There are records of attempts to burn the stones and then fracture them by tossing cold water on the hot surface. I set the scene at Christmas because it is a time when feelings would run high between opposing religions, and also to show a continuity of traditions that we associate with Christianity, but which are absorbed from origins much older. The Boar's Head Carol (associated with Oxford University, not far from Avebury) reflects the pre-Christian sacrificial meal of an animal both hated and revered for its fierceness and fearlessness. Carols themselves originally were circle dances, not just songs, and one of the old names for a Stone Circle is a "dance."

The contemporary naming day ceremony happened only in my imagination, and the people involved are fictional. However, I found a recent description of a Maypole dance held in the Circle and was told of modern naming and bonding ceremonies held there. The feast days and holy days of the "old religion" are regularly observed at Avebury by the current Keeper of the Stones and believers.

The upper parts of the River Kennet still disappear during the winter and reappear each spring. The scientific explanation involves the gradual emptying of a natural underground reservoir during the summer and its refilling during the winter rains, but the magical symbolism of death and rebirth still resonates.

Avebury Circle is interpreted by some archeologists as a place of celebration, in particular to symbolize the circle of life and death. Archeological remains seem to point to both harvest celebrations and funeral celebrations being held there. That is why I chose similar themes in my story.

I walked the Avenue toward the site of the Sanctuary, and the sense of grandeur present between the stones almost overwhelmed me. Little remains at the Sanctuary except an atmosphere of peace and a maze of concrete blocks marking post-holes, but current thought explores the idea that the sanctuary building was circular and open in the middle, like a donut.

Almost nothing remains of the second avenue (currently known as Beckhampton Avenue), and it seems to lead nowhere, so I took the liberty of using it as a ceremonial entrance for the stones themselves.

Silbury Hill remains a mystery. Tunnels and excavations have uncovered no tombs, not even that of King Sel, whom folklore links with the hill. But as I wrote the chapter in which Sel rides in a spiral to the summit, a friend sent me a newspaper clipping with the result of the latest dig — archeologists had uncovered traces of a spiral pathway to the summit!

As for the oak tree, it's always been known as a strong, long-lived, magical tree. This is reflected in English folklore and song, and English people are said to have hearts of oak.

Chantel, Adam, Holly and Owen will continue their quest through mystical England in Book Three, *The Heart of the Hill*.

Andrea Spalding

David Spalding

Award-winning author Andrea Spalding has written many popular books for children, including *Solomon's Tree,* illustrated by Janet Wilson and created in collaboration with Tsimpshian master carver Victor Reece; *Phoebe and the Gypsy*; *The Keeper and the Crows. The White Horse Talisman* (Book One in *The Summer of Magic Quartet*) has been nominated for the 2003 Silver Birch, Hackmatack and Manitoba Readers' Choice awards. An accomplished storyteller, Andrea hails from England, where she was long steeped in ancient lore. She now lives with her husband on Pender Island in British Columbia.

For more information about Andrea and her other publications, visit www.andreaspalding.com.

The Summer of Magic Quartet, Book One

Praise for *The White Horse Talisman*:

"This book . . . will have children of all ages dreaming of magic, enchantments and adventure." — *The Alan Review*

"Inventive, well paced and bursting with action . . . just right for middle-graders who love classic battles between good and evil." — *Booklist*

"*The White Horse Talisman* invites young readers on a fascinating foray into old English folklore and Celtic legends." — *CM Magazine*

⇨ Watch for Book Three in 2004, *Heart of the Hill*

Other books by Andrea Spalding

Solomon's Tree
illus. by Janet Wilson
1-55143-217-X; $19.95 cloth

It's Raining, It's Pouring
illus. by Leslie Elizabeth Watts
1-55143-229-3; $8.95 paper

Sarah May and the New Red Dress
illus. by Janet Wilson
1-55143-119-X; $8.95 paper

Me and Mr. Mah
illus. by Janet Wilson
1-55143-177-7; $8.95 paper

Phoebe and the Gypsy
1-55143-135-1; $6.95 paper

The Keeper and the Crows
1-55143-141-6; $6.95 paper